STARLIGHT

MR. MAC MEETS THE VESI

HARRY TRUMAN FLYNN

iUniverse, Inc.
New York   Bloomington

Starlight
Mr. Mac Meets the Vesi

iUniverse books may be ordered through booksellers or by contacting:

iUniverse
1663 Liberty Drive
Bloomington, IN 47403
www.iuniverse.com
1-800-Authors (1-800-288-4677)

ISBN: 978-1-4502-4600-2 (sc)
ISBN: 978-1-4502-4601-9 (dj)
ISBN: 978-1-4502-4602-6 (ebook)

Printed in the United States of America

iUniverse rev. date: 08/13/2010

I would like to acknowledge my wife, Irene, for her patience; my sister-in-law Joanne for her encouragement; and the Vesi civilization, from whom I hope we can someday adopt some of their philosophy and invent some of their technology.

Contents

Chapter One: Once Upon a Time

So. Here I am, in the middle of doing a mission for alien life forms and wondering if what I'm doing is right. I say alien, but in reality, they have been on Earth longer than humans have. I still refer to them as aliens, but I wish most of the time we humans could be more like them. I am a widower, and I know that my late wife, Karol, would have loved them. She loved to see people do the right thing and think of others. I miss her terribly, but I still have my work and the animals at home.

Maybe I should introduce myself. My name is George Washington MacAllister. I'm currently teaching astronomy to ninth and tenth graders at Treasure Coast High School in Vero Beach, Florida. I typically teach biology and earth science as well, but this year I only have four classes of astronomy students, three of which are honors students. The students, of course, refer to me as Big Mac, except in the classroom, where it's Mr. Mac. I am one of the middle-aged teachers. Think of a Dennis Quaid type with glasses and salt-and-pepper hair. I still believe a teacher should dress better than the students do, so I usually wear dress pants, shirt, and a tie. Of course, here in Florida, a jacket isn't usually necessary.

Vero Beach is located on the eastern coast of Florida. It is called the Treasure Coast because of all the Spanish ships that were sunk during hurricanes in the early eighteenth century, losing their cargos and crews. Their cargo was mainly Incan gold and silver going back to Spain. The Spaniards salvaged quite a bit of the treasure, but much of it is still here. The town of Vero Beach retains some of its old Florida charm, but now it is seeing more and more development as the population moves northward out of Miami.

This mission I was asked to do is not any kind of plot against mankind, governments, or anyone in particular. Some big mission, right? Well, for me, it is. I suppose I should tell you more about how this came about ... and what it is. Please remember that I am a teacher and not a professional writer, and sometimes I explain things in too much detail. So please be patient. Here goes.

It was a cold and rainy night. Wait, wrong story. Actually, it was a beautiful evening, and I was sitting on the sand dunes at Vero Beach, looking at the sky. Vero Beach is not a wide, flat beach like most in Florida; instead, it has rather steep dunes and a shorter beach. Karol and I used to walk up and down the beach and dunes and watch the people with metal detectors looking for some of the old "pieces of eight," as they are called. Occasionally, we saw someone actually find one, and he or she would be so excited and proud.

That evening, there was supposed to be a meteor shower, and Vero Beach was one of the best places for viewing, looking east with very little artificial light. The Atlantic Ocean was flat, with hardly a ripple. A thunderstorm had passed through in the afternoon, and everything was still. I was thinking back over the day at school and one of my astronomy classes in particular.

The school year had started several weeks earlier, and we were just getting into the formation of stars and planets and all the mechanics of the universe. We started with the "Big Bang," as it is called, or the "Big Flash," as I call it. We were discussing the development of the first electrons and protons from radiation into the formation of the first hydrogen atoms. Then the atoms grouped together to form clouds, and then the clouds grouped together to form protostars, protoplanets, and such.

"Then, when enough hydrogen had joined together by gravity to form a star, it would ignite into a nuclear fire and try to blast itself apart," I was explaining. "The star would try to collapse from gravity, so we ended up with a tug-of-war between gravity and expulsion. This continued until the hydrogen was exhausted enough for the star to collapse. The hydrogen was converted to helium and light was given off in the form of photons, creating a star. Our sun is one. The planets started forming at the same time, and we ended up with a solar system. We'll cover the physics of this later in the course. And don't worry—our sun isn't going to burn out for several billion years." A hand went up in the middle of the room. "Jonathan, you have a question?"

"Yes, Mr. Mac. I was told by someone that they were told the earth is only about ten thousand years old. How can that be?" Jonathan asked.

"Some religious leaders teach that, but we will not discuss or argue any religious ideas in this class," I said. "We will only go by the generally accepted scientific facts available at the present time. Remember that theories can and do change as knowledge increases. Up until 1947, it was said that machines could not possibly fly faster than the speed of sound. Chuck Yeager proved this wrong. The problem wasn't that the speed of sound couldn't be passed, but that the planes built at that time started coming apart from the vibrations created when hitting that speed. The X-1 was designed well enough to withstand this, and the rest is history."

I looked at one of the girls waving her hand. "Wanda, you have a question?"

"Did life originate soon after the earth was formed?" she asked.

"No," I replied. "To the best of our present scientific knowledge, the Big Flash happened about thirteen and a half to fifteen billion years ago. The Milky Way started forming about ten billion years ago, and our solar system and planets formed around four and a half to five billion years ago. The earth was not a friendly place at that time—it was very hot, with volcanoes everywhere, and there was hardly any oxygen. The air was mostly carbon dioxide, water vapor, and nitrogen. This has been called the Hadean period, from the Greek word Hades, or underworld, which we commonly refer to as hell. Sometime during the next billion years, after the earth had cooled somewhat, life started, evolving into microbes that could duplicate themselves. And later they started using sunlight for energy and CO_2, giving off oxygen as a waste product. This is called photosynthesis. Lucky for us, right? Most of this stuff will be covered in your biology class, so just take my word for now."

Another hand shot up. "Question, Brittany?"

"Did this happen all over the universe, or are we the only creatures anywhere?" the petite blonde asked.

"That's not a million-dollar question … but a many-trillions-of-dollars question," I replied. "Let me digress slightly and give you some info about that. In 1961, Frank Drake, a professor in California, developed an equation for estimating the number of intelligent civilizations in the Milky Way. The equation is $N = R \times fp \times ne \times fl \times fi \times fc \times L$."

The class was clearly now divided. About half looked interested or confused, and the rest seemed to be wishing they were somewhere else.

"Let me quickly explain this formula," I continued. "Bear with me, class, for a few minutes. We will discuss this in detail toward the end of the semester. The letters stand for the number of civilizations in our galaxy that we might expect to communicate with at any given time, the rate of star formation in the Milky Way, the fraction of stars that have planets, the average number of planets that can potentially support life per star if it has planets, and so forth and so on. Is your head about ready to explode? As I said, we'll get into this in more detail later. The numbers are all arguable, but for the sake of convenience, we'll just say that the result is in the billions or trillions universe-wide. Are UFOs real? Who knows? If one lands on the lawn someday, then we will know."

We continued the class as planned, and afterward, I decided to drive over to the dunes on the beach to see if any of the meteor shower was visible. The earth goes through meteor showers on a regular basis, and it's a beautiful sight to watch the "falling stars," especially when they are backlit by a very dark sky. Most of these objects are about the size of grains of sand or small pebbles, but they burn up when they find the friction of the earth's atmosphere and become quite visible. Larger ones can do real damage if they reach the surface. A few of the mass extinctions on Earth have been blamed on meteorite collisions. There is a lot of circumstantial evidence of this, but without proof, we can't know for sure. Meteor showers are mostly the debris from comets that come close to the earth, and we are going through the remnants of the tail. This is why the meteor showers are as predictable as the comets are.

The meteorites began to appear every few minutes, so I relaxed to enjoy the show.

Chapter Two: Meeting Milo

Around dusk, I spotted someone walking along the beach. Other than that, nobody else was around, which was great. However, it appeared that the person was headed straight toward me. I wasn't sure if I liked that or not. Lonely beach … single person … but then I noticed that he was smaller than I am, and he didn't look dangerous. He reminded me of Kevin Spacey, and he was casually dressed in slacks and a knit shirt. He had a smile on his face as he walked to where I was sitting.

"Hello, mind if I join you?" he said.

"Not at all. Are you here for the meteor shower also?" I asked.

"Actually, I'm here to talk to you," he replied. This gave me an uneasy feeling, and I looked at him more carefully to see if I knew him. I did not recognize him. Being a teacher, I met many parents, though.

"Do I know you? I don't seem to recall having met you."

"No, but I know you. You teach astronomy at Treasure Coast High, right?" he asked.

"Yes, I do," I said.

"This will take me awhile to explain. First, my name is Milo. Ever hear of a Milo?" he asked.

"Only in *Catch-22*," I replied.

"That's where I adopted my name from, but just the first name," he replied. "Anyway, I guess, as they used to say on Earth, 'Lucy, you got some 'splainin' to do.'" He then went on to say, "You had a discussion in class today about other life in the universe, correct?"

"That's right. Do you have a kid in my class?" I asked.

"No, but I was kind of in the classroom today … and most days, for that matter. I guess I had better start trying to explain myself," he said. "You see, I

5

am an alien to Earth, and I can tell there is some skepticism on your part … and rightly so." He paused as if waiting for a reaction.

I snickered slightly and studied him as if looking for scales, gills, or something that would give him, or *it*, away.

"Since this is Friday and you don't have to be in school until Monday, how would you like to go visit my place?" he asked. "I can give you a tour of my facilities."

Thinking this had to be a setup of some kind, I responded, "And where is this place of yours?"

"Out there," he replied, pointing to the ocean.

"On a boat?" I asked.

"No," Milo replied.

"On an island or Europe?" I asked skeptically.

"No, underwater," he said.

"Right!" I replied. "Do you also have some swampland you'd like to get rid of … or a Brooklyn Bridge, maybe?" I asked sarcastically.

"Up for a road trip, or should I say water ride?"

"Think I'll pass for now, but I'm sure you will have fun," I replied.

"If I can answer some personal questions about you, will you trust me?" he asked.

"Okay, I'll play," I said.

I looked away for a second to watch a meteor, and then I asked, "What's my wife's name?"

"It was Karol with a *K*, but she died last year from cancer after twenty-nine years of marriage," Milo confidently said.

"Yes, but you could have read that in the paper," I said.

"Okay, you have a five-year-old dog named Ralph, and two cats named Hide and Seek. Was that in the paper? You never had any children. You love seafood and listen to mostly oldies from the fifties through the seventies—my favorites also," Milo stated.

I was surprised. Those things were not common knowledge or found in any newspaper.

"Where is your boat, then?" I quizzed.

"Boat? Boats don't go underwater on purpose!" he said.

"Then where's your sub?"

"Do you want to go?" Milo asked.

By this time, I was actually getting interested, although every bit of common sense and intelligence told me this was a setup and Milo was a kook.

"What the hell," I responded. "Life isn't that exciting—not by myself anyway."

He looked up and down the beach and then out toward the Atlantic. He said something like "Bebop, debeep, splong."

Suddenly, out over the deeper part of the ocean, I saw what looked like a black flattened cylinder about twelve feet high by about twenty feet across. It was gliding toward the shore with no sound of any kind. I couldn't see any seams, doors, or windows at all. It stopped on the beach, and a door opened in the outer surface of the craft. I was hesitant to get in. I stopped and thought about what I had seen, and in the name of science, I had to check this out.

There was little interior light until we were inside and the door closed. There were no sounds at all from the boat or sub or UFO or whatever we were in. All the walls were lit up with gauges, dials, and screens, and there was a joystick-type control on a console. There were five chairs around the console, and looking at the screens, I saw that there were views from everywhere outside. The screens looked like they were windows on the sides of the craft, but from outside, I'd seen no indication of windows, so I was assuming they were screens.

All the writing was in a language that looked like a cross between Arabic, Greek, and hieroglyphics. I wanted to ask questions, but I didn't know where to start. Milo motioned for me to sit in one of the seats. When I did, it adjusted to me like a glove, and restraints went around my lap and chest, self-adjusting so they felt custom made. This scared me a little, but they weren't too snug, and my hands and arms were free, so I wasn't captive.

"Dedonk, donk," said Milo, and we started slowly moving. There was still no sound, but I could feel the acceleration. We sped up for a few minutes and then slowed, starting slowly into the Atlantic. I grabbed the armrests and gulped.

Milo said, "Any questions now?"

"Yes, who's driving, or flying, or navigating? Whatever we are doing …"

"The ship is on what I guess you would call autopilot—for lack of a better word at this time—since I told it to take us to my place."

"Okay, I'll bite. Where's your place?" I inquired.

"Not far. Just in the Puerto Rican Trench, around twenty-eight thousand feet down," he replied.

"No vessel has gone that deep and had any survivors," I said. "Only small unmanned subs make that trek."

"I know," he replied. "That's why we live there."

"We?"

"Wait a few minutes and everything will be perfectly vague," he said.

"That's what scares me," I said.

The gauges or meters, or whatever they were, were busy changing symbols, but I couldn't understand any of the characters being displayed. The view was like one you would see in a sub with a large bubble nose. Even though we were surrounded by water, there wasn't a lot of sea life around.

The trip was interesting since I had no idea where we were or how deep. There was no indication that we were going deeper because I would have expected to have either felt something or heard the hull of the vessel make noises or something. I know the pressure causes things to crush, but I heard nothing, not even engine noises. It was eerily quiet. There were some sounds other than the water, but they were hard to explain. In just a few minutes, we were near the bottom, but just how deep, I couldn't tell. Then I saw a few tube worms and thermal vents in the screens or windows. We dropped down into a valley or trench and stopped a little above the bottom. A door in the side of the wall of the trench opened from the top, similar to a garage door. The door hadn't been visible until it rose. The vessel went inside, and the door closed. I heard the sound of air rushing in around the vessel and water leaving. It took about thirty seconds for the entire chamber to empty of water, and it looked completely dry. You could see the water level drop through the panels. Milo then said something like "Gedope, billig," but I didn't know whom he was talking to.

Suddenly, the door of our craft opened, and Milo said, "Follow me and don't be afraid. This is going to be the most exciting weekend of your life."

I was starting to get the feeling that this was some kind of government or military operation. We walked into the chamber where the water had been, and I touched the walls. They were bone dry.

"How did you do that?" I asked.

"Later," he replied. "First I need you to meet some folks."

Another door opened. I noticed that all the doors slid into the walls from the center, except for the door through which we came into this hangar, or whatever it was, from the ocean. We stepped into what looked like a huge laboratory, and it contained numerous consoles and screens. With its flasks, machines, lab equipment, and various other things I couldn't identify, it looked like a combination of a chemistry lab and an electronics lab. There were charts, screens, and other things on the walls, but I couldn't really describe them, and I didn't see a single word I recognized. And then I saw them—about twenty beings looking a lot like the "grays" that people had claimed to be abducted by.

My pounding heart was about to break my ribs, and I was scared. They were of various sizes, as any group of humans would be. They had large almond-shaped coal black eyes with no pupils that I could see. Their heads were larger than human heads, with only holes on the sides for ears. Their mouths were small in comparison to ours, but they were closed so I couldn't see anything in the way of teeth. Their noses were small rounded bumps with two nostrils mostly open toward the front. Their skin color was a dull gray, and they had short grayish hair and no eyebrows. I noticed that they only had two fingers and a thumb on each hand.

They all stopped what they were doing and stared blankly at me with those big blackish eyes, not saying a word. I started wondering if I was going to be lunch. Milo was silent. Just when I got up the nerve to say something like "Hello" or "What the hell are you?" one and then another and another started laughing, and soon the entire group was laughing. Then they all took off their heads and the gloves they were wearing, and I saw that they had normal-human looking heads and hands, and they appeared to be of all ethnic backgrounds. They all smiled, and after a few moments, they returned to what they were doing.

"I've been had?" I asked.

"Only sort of. You see, we are aliens … but I will explain it all this weekend if you'd like to stay. Otherwise, I can take you back to the beach or home."

"What if I told everyone?" I asked.

"And what institution would they put you in?" he asked.

"Is this a military or government operation?" I asked.

"No. I can tell you for sure that neither the government nor the military have any idea about anything you will see this weekend. They are working on a few things you will see, but they are at least decades, if not forever, away from discovery," he said. "Does this sound like something you might be interested in discovering?" he added.

"What about my animals? I need to look after them," I said.

"You can ask your neighbor Troy to go over and take care of them, or I can call a service to take care of them."

"Let me call Troy and ask him if he'll go over. Since Karol passed, he usually does it for me when I have to go out of town."

"Fine," he said. "We have surface phones hooked up over here. Your cell phone is not usable down here."

I called Troy and asked him if he would look after Ralph and Hide and Seek since I had a school emergency out of town. He had a key and was very reliable. He readily agreed to help.

"Thanks, Troy. I'll see you when I get back," I said, hanging up.

"What about my car?" I asked Milo. "It won't be safe out there all night."

"We will have it moved to the school and parked there, if that's all right," Milo said.

"Sure," I replied.

"Are you getting hungry yet?" Milo asked.

"I could eat. What do you people eat? Humans?" I asked.

"No, you all are too stringy." He chuckled, smiled, and said, "Just kidding. We don't eat intelligent species. We eat the same things you do. We eat a lot of fish. We like fish since our home planet had only one continent, about the size of North America, and the rest was ocean. I'll explain a lot at dinner tonight. Let's go up and order something."

"Go up where?" I asked.

"Up where it isn't so deep," he said. "We have an elevator. Follow me."

We walked to a door, it opened , and we went inside. It was about the size of a normal elevator, except it was round instead of square. There were no floor buttons, as you would expect to see in an elevator, or anything that I assumed was for communicating. Milo said something I couldn't understand, and the elevator started up. It was going so fast that I could feel the force of gravity, but it made no sounds at all. We slowed, stopped, and got out, and there was a large window or screen, I'm still not sure which, looking into the ocean. I could see a few fish and other creatures swimming by.

"How deep are we?" I asked

"About two hundred feet or so," Milo replied. He went over to a smallish box and said something into it. "I'm calling Sam," he said.

In a few minutes, a big male dolphin appeared at the window and starting making dolphin sounds, which were coming out of the box that Milo had spoken into. These were a combination of pops, clicks, squeaks, and squeals, which I had heard before on nature programs.

"Just a minute," Milo said into the box. "English on."

The dolphin started making noises again, but I now heard English coming out of the box. "Who's the walker?" I heard.

"Maybe I should explain," Milo said, turning to me. "We have been communicating with dolphins and whales for millions of years. The box will translate anything they say to any language known on Earth—and some not of this world." Milo appeared to be waiting for my look of disbelief.

"Sam just asked who you are. He refers to humans as walkers, except for tuna fishermen. I can't really say all the things he says about them." Then, as he turned to the box, he said, "Sam, this is Mr. MacAllister, my weekend guest and a science teacher. He is a good walker and has a genuine love for creatures."

This was either the most elaborate hoax or the real thing.

"Nice to meet you," Sam said.

"Where did you get the name Sam?" I asked. "I thought all you dolphins were named Flipper." I was gently laughing.

He laughed as well. "My name, Sam, stands for superior aquatic mammal—picked it myself."

"What looks good tonight, Sam?" Milo asked.

"Tuna is the best today. A large school has been going by most of the day. Would you like one?" Sam asked.

"Sure, about a five pounder, if you don't mind," Milo said.

"That small isn't even a challenge," Sam said. "I can get much bigger."

"That will be plenty—it's just the two of us tonight," Milo said.

"Be back in less than four minutes. Time me. Ready, set, go." Sam disappeared into the deep.

"Is Sam trained?" I asked.

"Not a bit more than any other dolphin in the ocean," Milo said. "The translator box speaks dolphin to him and whatever language we want to us."

A few minutes later, Sam went by the window with a tuna, looking as if he was making a victory lap. He then placed it in an opening in the wall.

"Thanks," Milo said.

"Sam," I said. "Can you do me a favor? Would you spin three times for me?"

"The walker is a nonbeliever, ha-ha," Sam said, starting to spin and counting as he did so.

"Now I'm convinced. You have to realize that this is all new to me," I remarked. "Sam, may I ask a few questions?"

"Sure," Sam said.

"Do you communicate with whales?" I asked.

"On occasion we talk, but not much. Their language is different from ours. You would say theirs is more like singing. They have a smaller vocabulary, but the way they sing is a lot like facial expressions for walkers. There is a lot of information in the pitch, speed, and duration. Why do you ask?"

"Do they know about the captive whales in places like Sea World and the like?"

"Yes, they can communicate with them through low-frequency vibrations in the ground and water," Sam replied.

"What do they think of the situation?" I inquired.

"They have mixed feelings. They are well cared for, but they are still captive. They think that possibly this is the only way their species can survive. If they were given a choice, though, they would all return to the open ocean and take their chances," Sam continued.

"Thanks a lot for the information. I may want to talk some more at some other time. Is that all right, Sam?"

"As they say in the Gulf of Mexico, no problemo and bon appétit." Sam took off.

Milo motioned me to follow him, saying it was time to go eat the tuna Sam brought us. We passed several things that looked like doors with signs that appeared to be nice LCDs or plasma. They were not dots but actual symbols. It again looked like a cross between Arabic, Greek, and hieroglyphics. I could not read anything and decided Milo would let me know if it was important.

We went into what looked like a fancy restaurant, and a host greeted me as Mr. MacAllister and also greeted Milo. He showed us to our table, which was set as nicely as any first-class restaurant table on the surface. We sat down, and a server came over and said our tuna was being prepared. He asked if we would like a drink and appetizer.

I replied that I sure could use a scotch and water, if possible, and Milo asked for an extra-dry martini. Milo also asked the server if he would pick a good white wine to go with dinner, and he replied that he would be delighted to do that.

"What brand of scotch do you normally drink?" our waiter asked. His name tag was again in the language I could not read.

"Chivas Regal, if you have it," I replied.

"The twelve or the twenty-one-year-old Salute?"

"The twelve," I replied, having tried the Salute; it was too malty for me. Besides, I couldn't afford it on a teacher's salary.

I looked around the place for a few minutes, and Milo was silent. I think he was trying to watch my reactions.

"What would you like to know first?" Milo asked.

"Let's start with where you get your food."

"There are several thousand of us here most of the time, so that requires a lot of food," he said. "Except for seafood, which we usually catch ourselves, we get it on the surface, just as you do, by buying it. We eat most of the same things you do, except we have to have supplements that aren't available on Earth, and we make those ourselves. There are about a hundred thousand of us on the surface, and some of them spend a lot of time buying supplies and selling things to get money. On the surface, we have people in the grocery business, metal business, and practically every other legal business. We don't have any people in big decision-making positions because it is against our charter and beliefs to influence humans as a group. We don't have anyone in government, law enforcement, education, or practicing medicine, like doctors or nurses. We only interact on this level with selected individuals, and I'll explain how you either got lucky, or unlucky, as you may perceive it."

"What types of things do you sell on the surface to buy things?" I asked.

"Mostly metals we pick up or extract from the ocean," Milo said. "There is a lot of gold in seawater, but you have to know how to filter it out. It takes an electronic filter set to a certain frequency. We also make artificial diamonds, but we do not cut and polish them. We just make the crystals and sell them. We only do small ones so as not to attract much attention. We've been here a long time, as I will explain later, and we live a lot longer, as I will also explain later. I bet you really feel like a student now. Think of this as a field trip."

Somehow, I knew this was going to be a long weekend.

Our server brought us our meal, and it looked delicious. One bite and I was sure it was the best tuna I had ever tasted. The wine was poured, and it was wonderful as well. I wondered what the protocol was for this place. Did we pay or what?

"Are the workers here part of your group?" I asked.

Milo laughed and said, "Yes, you're the only human here at this time. I probably need to explain how we work here. We take turns doing things. One week I might be a waiter, and the next week I might be a researcher. There is no set schedule for how long you do something, and no jobs are more important than others. If there's something you like to do more than others, you can work at it longer. We sign up for positions, and some jobs require extra training and are not available to everyone, but if you want, you can get training. Of course, sometimes there are physical restrictions with the jobs. Some people have been in their jobs for centuries."

"Wait. For *centuries*?" I asked.

"Maybe I'll explain. I planned on doing this later but what the heck. As I said, we live a lot longer than people on Earth normally do. We live between four and five hundred years—Earth years, that is."

"We have eliminated practically all diseases and disorders through genetic research," he continued. "We don't reproduce in exactly the same fashion as humans, and we seldom get any Earth diseases due to a genetic difference that we will go through later."

"I've got to find out about all of this. Do you realize how much money could be made from some of this technology?" I said excitedly.

"That's another difference; we have no use for money, for the most part."

"But you buy and sell things and conduct other commerce on the surface," I said.

"Yes, we do. That's because we have to be able to interact with humans. You're a money-based race.

"Do you want to find out about us?" he asked. "You were singled out for a small mission. It's strictly on a volunteer basis, and you will learn more and see things that no human has seen before—and it will be centuries before anyone else sees them. Sound interesting?"

"I'm getting more confused," I replied.

"I know there's a lot to absorb, but first I'd like to do something to make things easier for you to understand us and communicate," Milo said. "All our signs here are a type of crystal display that uses almost no power, but they're in our native language. There's a device that you can carry, or it can be implanted, that will cause the signs to change to English or whatever language the device is programmed for. The technology is smaller than nanotechnology; it is more picotechnology."

"Implanted? You mean like an RFID chip?" I asked.

"Pretty much, except it actually does more. It will also let us know where you are at all times, like a GPS sender but a lot better. You will have to take my word for it for now. I would show you one but you can't see it with the naked eye, only with an extremely high-powered microscope. This is getting complicated, isn't it?" he asked.

"Yes. How do you implant it?" I inquired.

"With a hypodermic. We can also implant devices that will translate any language into English for you. There are two of them, one for each ear, and they are implanted close to the nerves from your ears. They intercept impulses and recognize them as language. Then they translate them and send the impulses as English," he explained.

"Right! And now the swampland!" I replied.

Milo responded, "You will have to see some of our technology before you will believe."

"How long have you guys been here on Earth?" I inquired.

"The short answer is about four billion years. The long answer will take a lot longer to explain. We were not able to live here without suits at first, so we only visited until the atmosphere became oxygenated and life started," Milo went on.

"I know ... I'll find out later, right?" I asked.

"Yes. The implants can be removed later if you prefer, but they will assist in your understanding of things for now. If you agree, what I would like to do is have them installed while you are asleep tonight because we are going to have a busy day tomorrow, as we have to take a few little trips. You'll never even know they are there—except that you will understand every language on Earth. But you still won't be able to speak it without learning it. So far, we've never been able to get that to work. The brain is just too complicated for even our technology."

I thought for a minute and replied, "Why not?"

Milo motioned our waiter over, ordered two Cognacs, and told the waiter to touch up mine because I was going to join them for the weekend. I assumed he meant for him to spike my drink so I would sleep soundly. The waiter returned with a small capsule in his hand and said he wanted me to see how it worked. I looked at his name tag, which read Carl.

"Is that the device?" I asked.

"Yes," Carl said. "Watch my nametag. English off." His name tag returned to the scribble it was before. "English on," he said, and it returned to Carl.

"Try it yourself," he said.

"English off," I said, and the scribble returned. "English on." The name Carl returned to the name tag. It could be a parlor trick but I would take my chances.

"Is this capsule what you implant?" I asked.

They both laughed, and Milo said, "No, it is in there, but you can't see it. I mean, you can't physically see it because it is so small, not that there is anything secret about it. By the way, we have *no* secrets from you because you could go to the surface and tell everyone and nobody, but nobody would believe you until we are ready to make our presence known to the race—if it lasts long enough. This will be a lot clearer by time the weekend is over, I promise."

We had our Cognac, and Milo led me to a room, saying I was free to call anyone on the phone. He said he thought I might want to check on Ralph and Hide and Seek.

The room looked like one in a first-class hotel. I still wasn't sure if this was real or an elaborate setup, but I didn't know anyone rich enough to pull it off, or anyone who would want to.

There was a box on the wall, about forty inches across, and it looked like a television without the screen. There was a remote, so I picked it up and pointed toward the box. It came to life. It was a holographic-type television. I could see what looked like real things inside it. Looking at the remote, I noted that the panel was flat except for what looked like buttons traced out on it. None of them were labeled.

I thought for a minute and said, "English on." All the labels appeared in English. "English off." They went blank. "French on." They came on in French. "Russian on," I said, and they started alternating between French and Russian. "English on." They started alternating between French, Russian, and English. When I said, "French off; Russian off," only English appeared. I started scanning through channels and guessed that every television channel in the world was on it. They were all holographic. It actually was a little scary seeing what looked like a miniature person talking. I wasn't sure humans were ready for holographic television just yet. On the remote, there was a button marked 2D. I pushed it, and the TV reverted to a two-dimensional screen. I felt relieved. Looking at someone's head in the box was disturbing.

I started getting sleepy and found everything in the bathroom I needed, including my own brands of toothpaste, deodorant, and mouthwash. They also had the same brand of toilet paper I used. This was a little bit unnerving, but I'm sure it was done with all good intentions. These people seemed to be genuine. These people! I didn't even know what to call them yet.

The bed looked like a normal bed, but when I lay down, it was extremely comfortable. I went to sleep almost immediately. I don't remember any dreams, if I had any. A short while later, I awoke feeling rested. I showered and wondered if someone would come get me. I looked in the closet, and there were new clothes, in my style and the correct size, of course. These could have been taken from my closet, if it weren't for the fact they were new. When I'd gotten out of the shower, there was a pot of coffee waiting for me, and it was my brand. These people could make a billion on the surface. My local newspaper was on the table, and I spent about thirty minutes reading it to see if I could find anything about alien abductions, but there was nothing.

There was a knock on the door. "Come in," I said. It was Milo, and he seemed excited.

"Going to be a fun and exciting day, Mr. Mac," he said.

"Just make it Mac or George," I said.

"I like Mac, Mac," he said. "Let's go get something to eat and get started."

"Sounds like a plan to me," I said. We went to a cafeteria-like place and I noticed that when I walked in, the signs were in gibberish, but as I neared them, they changed to English. The nametags all read English when I was close. "What if one of you needs the sign in your language, what do you do?"

"We tell it to come on in our language. Like this. Vesi bedonk," he said, and it blinked slowly between English and scribble. I noticed it changed and stopped reading in English when I got farther away. We found a place to sit, and many people were having all kinds of breakfasts, from rolls to fully prepared meals. They seemed to be having a good time, but I couldn't understand anything they said.

When we sat down, Milo said, "We need to try out your translators. You need to say, 'Right ear on.' Block your left ear," he added.

"Right ear on," I repeated, and I began hearing everyone speaking English on my right side. I unplugged my left ear and it was still gibberish. Boy, was that confusing. "Left ear on," I said, before Milo could say anything, and all I heard was English.

"Very good," said Milo. "We knew you were a quick study."

"What do I call you people?" I inquired.

"We are called Vesi or the Vesi," Milo said. "One is a Vesi, two are Vesi, and one hundred trillion are Vesi. Maybe we should stop by the history room so I can give you the twenty-five-cent tour. You can fill in details later if you wish. We may have to delay our road trips until next weekend since it looks like we may get a little busy."

"Good idea. I'm still a little foggy about all this. You know, it isn't every day that you get abducted," I joked.

"Correction, Mac. You came willingly and are free to return at any time," Milo said.

"Just kidding. I'm just starting to believe that it's truly real. Let the fun begin!"

As we finished eating, I asked numerous small questions, but every time I asked something more complex, Milo just told me "later" or said to wait until we got someplace.

I decided that if they wanted me to know, they would tell me. I was wondering why I was picked to see this, but I didn't want to inquire too much, for fear they might change their minds.

Chapter Three: History Lesson

We walked for a while, and I asked Milo about some of their operations. I was surprised to find out that there were more places like this on Earth. Almost all oceans on Earth had one or more. They also didn't allow any of their technology to go topside, except their craft when they traveled, and they tried to hold that to a minimum.

"Are there other visitors besides the Vesi here on Earth?" I asked.

"We'll talk in detail later about that," he answered.

Every answer brought on ten more questions. We went into a theater-size room, which probably *was* a theater since it had a large box like my television up in the front and rows of seats facing the box. We sat down, and Milo asked me to wait until the presentation was over, saying he would then answer any questions. The room darkened, and at the same time, the box came to life with what looked like a galaxy in a holographic viewer. It was a spiral galaxy much like the Milky Way.

"This is our home galaxy," Milo said. "Somewhere near the center is our home solar system. I mean, *was* our home solar system. After the Big Bang, our galaxy was one of the first to form. That was about twelve billion years ago. It is smaller than the Milky Way, but our sun was larger. Our planet, Vesi, was slightly larger than Earth, but we were farther away, so we had a similar climate. We had two moons that would be about the same mass as Earth's moon if they were combined.

"Oxygen-dependent life forms started and evolved, and you know the drill," Milo went on. "Our star, being larger of course, was burning out faster than your sun will. We realized our sun was going nova on us, and we had to leave.

"The lucky thing for us was that we never went through the hydrocarbon fuel stage that Earth is presently in. We had very little petroleum, and it was only used for things like lubricants and plastics. We went from animal transportation, a lot like horses but much smellier, straight to electric-powered vehicles. We had, in a short time, all transportation controlled by computers, and driving was not normally needed. At first, we drove ourselves, but there were too many accidents and traffic congestion. We quickly developed nuclear power and then gravitational propulsion.

"That's what we still use. Gravity, the Big G, is the most powerful thing we have discovered in the universe so far. Gravity is the weakest of the forces, but it uses mass to multiply itself. There are so many things about gravity that we still don't understand and are still working on, but it is available everywhere, clean, and free. Every particle in the universe uses gravity in one way or another.

"Anyway, we needed to leave, and the next planet out from us, your Mars equivalent, also had life on it, but none had developed higher intelligence and communications, so we were on our own. We were the only intelligent species on Vesi, and we had developed through only a few lines. With our gravity-powered craft, we—and when I say 'we,' I don't mean *me*, just my distant ancestors—sent out robot scout craft all over the universe."

I noticed that the viewer switched to robot craft being sent out. These looked like small saucer-shaped craft with lots of antennae on them.

"There is a method of travel by gravity that is a lot like *Star Trek*'s warp speed, and we discovered it by accident. We found that every particle in the universe knows where every other particle is. How, we still don't know, but there are ways to jump from place to place. We have millions of them mapped out. It was trial and error. By setting our mass to a certain level and going where it took us, we could map it, return, and change settings to go somewhere else. Once we got that spot all figured out, we'd go to one of the destinations and start all over again. We even had robot craft do this for a couple of million years, and we made pretty good maps."

The viewer showed maps that looked like big star charts. There were many stars of various sizes, and most had symbols next to them. At the bottom was a legend with much more information. I could not read any of them.

"Speaking of years, remember I told you that we live four or five hundred years. A lot of the reason is because our planet was farther away from our sun, and our years were longer, and then genetic manipulation accounts for about half. Still following?" he asked.

"So far, I have no reason, except my own earthly skepticism, to doubt you," I replied. "This is all new uncharted territory for me. I feel like Columbus right now."

"Wait until you find out about him. Lucky devil he was!" Milo said.

The viewer had focused in on a beautiful rose-like supernova. The color was a deep red, with petals that looked like waves coming out of the center.

"Anyway, our sun did go nova, and our whole solar system went out of existence, but we were scattered around lots of other habitable planets. We still communicate with each other using dark energy communication systems. Dark energy is instantaneous over distances, and we still don't know the processes fully. Here on Earth, the speed of light is theoretically the limit that anything can travel. One of the reasons is the limited speed of electricity used in your instruments. If you had instruments capable of detecting things faster than light, you might be surprised at what goes on in the universe."

Milo changed the viewer, and a couple of galaxies appeared. Then the dark void of space filled with a light blue color. Milo said, "The blue represents dark matter. Of course, it isn't blue and visible, but this is for demonstration purposes. It is everywhere, and it seems to be more concentrated closer to galaxies and planets and anything visible in the universe."

I did notice that the color was a little more intense around the galaxies. "Dark energy and dark matter are just now being theorized," I said. "We aren't even sure if it exists, but we have no other explanation for how things appear. Dark matter seems to make up most of the universe. Why isn't it visible? It appears we can see its effects on gravity but can't see it," I added.

Milo replied, "This is the Cliff Notes version of dark matter and dark energy, as explained to me by some of our scientists. Everything in the universe that we know of is energy. Actually, there is no such thing as matter. Matter is composed of energy in different forms. The smallest particles we have ever discovered are made of energy. Electrons, protons, neutrons, and the things that make them, quarks, and the things that make quarks, and the things that make those particles are all just energy. We have yet to find the smallest particle, but we are on a quest to find what would be the God particle in human terms. There seem to be as many small divisions as there are large divisions. We are just getting close to the edge of the known universe and will probably find a much larger something there. I will have some of the Vesi that are studying this in depth go over it with you."

While he was speaking, the viewer had switched to Earth, with one supercontinent, Pangaea, growing out of numerous minor continents. The viewer then showed land animals similar to large lizards walking around.

"Soon after land animals came into existence, we started coming here to possibly live, and it looked as if we were going to have a planet like Vesi, with just one continent on it. But it didn't exactly turn out that way, as you know. Making a long story short, we were physically an awful lot like humans, but there were some differences. A few hundred million years ago, we learned how to manipulate our DNA, and yes, we have DNA, but it is different, as you will find out. We learned how to duplicate the looks of the evolving creatures that were turning out to be intelligent. We made many mistakes but finally got good control, and we can now make our replacements to order. This is different from cloning.

"Several thousands of years ago, we realized we needed to find someplace to hide, and we ended up building these places. Why? You see, our objective is not to conquer worlds but to study them. We have never been in a war, and we have no government, just our people. All our people are of the same mind-set, and finding out about the universe and what else there might be is our mission. Don't be upset, but humans are just another species for us to try to understand. A lot like how humans study the animals below them. We aren't saying we are better, just technically more advanced and more curious."

Milo showed me many other holographic images of worlds, galaxies, and supernova, and I watched them while he explained what was going on. They were fascinating. There were planets that looked similar to Earth and some that looked like giant snowballs. There were galaxies like the Milky Way and several with other shapes. The supernovas were just tremendous. There would be an enormous star, and everything looked peaceful. Then there was a sudden extreme bright flash, and the star was blown to bits. Since I had always loved explosions, this was the holy grail of explosions. I was just awed by everything and so excited that I had been chosen to see it.

It was time for lunch by then, and we went to a cafeteria. Milo said we would go try out the time machine after lunch. This I had to see! A time machine was what half the science fiction readers and writers always dreamed about. Although, when I thought about it, it could be dangerous. Was it real? Has it ever been used with humans? Did it hurt? Another adventure!

Chapter Four: The Time Machine

We walked down a few halls, and I couldn't help but wonder how large this place was—or was it similar to the rides at Disney World that just kept looping back and forth? When I asked Milo how big it was, he said he would prefer just to say "very large" for now. We then entered a room that looked as big as an aircraft hangar. The only thing in the room was a console in the middle of the floor. There were also a couple of stools. I couldn't see any computers or controls, only a joystick-looking thing in the center of the console.

We walked over to the console, and Milo opened a panel and took out what looked like a couple of stainless steel metal kitchen bowls with chinstraps and a couple of eye covers. He told me to sit on the left stool and put on the eyeshades and the transporter cover over my head. It wasn't connected to anything, but from the technology that I had seen, I wasn't surprised. I couldn't see anything, and I was anxious. What if this didn't work with humans and I ended up in the middle of a star or turned into moss or something?

"This has been tried with humans, right?" I asked.

"Yes, of course," Milo responded.

"Was everything all right?" I went on.

"We think so," Milo said.

"Think so!" I said.

"Just kidding. They will probably be back in a couple of years," he added. "No, really, there is no danger. Trust me."

Milo said, "For our first trip, we are taking a little journey back to the Jurassic period. You will be able to see just how accurate the scientists and anthropologists have been in their conclusions. First we are going to the time when the dinosaurs were having their best days, and then later, we'll go to when things got really bad and they became extinct. Sound good?"

"I'll know when we get there. Does this hurt?" I asked.

"You won't feel a thing or hear a thing. Just sit back and relax," Milo said.

I put the eye covers and the helmet thing on. I heard Milo pressing some buttons, but I didn't feel anything. However, I began to notice a musty smell.

"Go ahead and remove your cover and eyeshades and be ready for some excitement," Milo said.

At this time, I was so anxious that I didn't know if I would be able to contain myself. What if it was real and we got injured while we were there? I removed the cover and eyeshades and was hardly able to speak. I saw a bunch of dinosaurs about a hundred yards ahead and some smaller ones closer. The first thing I noticed about them was their colors. The larger ones were mostly gray, and some were greenish and looked almost camouflaged. Some of the smaller ones, about turkey size, were colorful and had crests and what looked like small feathers. Some of the larger ones were eating various fern-like plants, and some were sitting down on the ground as dogs or cows do. I saw what looked like a mammal scurrying through the forest from plant to plant. It was about the size of a possum and actually looked a lot like one except it had more fur. The hair was thick but not like that of a porcupine. The musty smell was a lot like what you smell around a swamp. The only trees that I saw looked a lot like palms crossed with ferns. I didn't know where to start. I was glad to see the console was still there.

"How is this possible?" I asked Milo.

"Go over and touch that tree over there and learn the secret," Milo said.

I walked about ten feet over to the tree and reached out to touch it. I mean, I tried to touch the tree. My hand went through it, and I felt nothing.

"This isn't real, is it?" I asked.

"It was. It's a hologram that was recorded during the time we are supposed to be experiencing. We have been recording for hundreds of millions of years and have a large library from when the earth was not habitable until the present. We have recording technology that records from so many angles that you can actually go up close to look at Mr. T-Rex in total safety. Believe me, we've tried to go back to the past, but we've never been able to. Anyway, you just need to know that we use the thing you call a joystick to move around. Any questions now?" Milo asked.

"Then where does the smell come from?" I asked.

"Good question," said Milo. "We started recording sight, sound, smells, and temperatures many millions of years ago. That was a real technical advance at the time," he added.

"Next question. What was the cover I had on my head?"

"What did it look like?" he asked.

"It looked like a kitchen mixing bowl," I said.

"Again, you are right. I thought up that little extra touch. You'll discover that we like to have fun as long as no one gets harmed. We'll be having more fun before long," he said. "We discovered universe-wide that the more intelligent civilizations are, the better sense of humor they have. This doesn't mean playing tricks all the time, but being able to see humor even in bad times is a real survival instinct. Besides, we haven't been able to understand why some people would want to survive anyway if they hate everything about life so much."

He switched gears. "How do you like our hologram system?"

"I love it, and if I had it a year, I'd be the richest person on Earth," I replied.

"Is that your goal? To be the richest person on Earth?"

I thought for a few seconds and replied, "Guess not or I never would have gone into teaching."

"I agree," Milo said. "Let's go look at dino and friends."

He took the joystick, and we went right up to the dinosaurs. They did not smell good, and I saw that there was dino doo-doo all around. They seemed so real. The sounds were somewhat low and they seemed to be communicating gently with each other. Then I saw some small ones in the center of the group. It was as if they were protecting them. Right then, I was glad they were not real—or perhaps I should say "alive." Milo motioned for me to take the control, and I asked if there was anything I should be aware of. He said just to go slow until I got used to it. I started going forward, and by instinct, I went around the group. Although I could go through it, it just didn't seem right to do that. They seemed so peaceful and content.

"I'm sure you want to see a *T. rex*," Milo said.

"I'm game since I can't be lunch," I replied.

"Let me input some coordinates in the console here, and we'll have a good view of one hunting." He typed something into the console. I couldn't read it because the console did not change to English. I figured that maybe I would ask about this later. Suddenly, the entire landscape changed, and we were about fifty yards from a *T. rex*. He, I think it was a he—yep, I could see that it was a male—started moving quickly toward a dinosaur lying on the ground. With his small beady eyes and large mouth and teeth, the *T. rex* was frightening. He was very loud, and the ground almost shook when he moved and made noise. His coloring was different than I had imagined. He was blotchy with browns, grays, and greens. These colors were randomized and went from almost a black to a light green. The colors were brighter on the neck and head, and there were dark patches around the eyes. These made the eyes look larger than they really were. The small birdlike creatures feeding on the dead dino were much more colorful, with some reds and blues and bright greens. I thought those bird things were going to be lunch. Wrong! He scared them off so he could have the carcass.

"I'll be damned!" I exclaimed.

"So would most people," Milo said. "*T. rex* was a scavenger, but he had the equipment to totally dismantle any creature. He would occasionally take a smaller dino or a mammal if it got close enough, but as noisy as they were, only the sick or injured ones weren't scared off."

There was a loud snap of breaking bones as the *T. rex* took a large bite out of the carcass.

"Holy mackerel!" I exclaimed. Milo just smiled.

"We believe they made noise to scare other dinosaurs off. They didn't seem to want to fight. The short arms were useless for fighting. They were almost cold-blooded. The smaller dinosaurs, the birdlike ones, were actually warm-blooded and a lot more active. The good news is we have complete creatures preserved and a total DNA archive starting from when the earth was not habitable.

"We have always been interested in DNA since we discovered it and learned how to manipulate it," he continued. "Guess that's what you do when you don't want to spend all your resources killing each other. I think we never had those problems since we only had one continent and everyone was somewhat equal. It's the same reason we never developed many government-type organizations."

"Let's go find some of your distant relatives," he said. "We will start back when the first land animals came ashore."

He cued in something on the console, and we were at the seashore. There were some ugly-looking creatures close to the shore. This was not your typical beach but instead was a lagoon just off the beach. You could hear the waves crashing in the distance, but the water here was relatively calm. You could smell the ocean, but there were many other smells mixed in. It was like a brackish water smell. It was a little swampy, with a hint of sulfur. There were some creatures about a foot long wiggling around the mud and going back into the water. They looked like walking catfish, kind of like the ones we have in Florida. There were some large insects flying around, and they looked like dragonflies. As they landed near the mud, occasionally one of the creatures would wiggle out and more or less walk on its fins and grab one. It gulped air, and I realized that this was the start of lunged creatures. It was desolate except around the water's edge. There were fernlike plants around but not a great variety of them.

"Fast forward a few hundred million years and see what's going on," Milo said.

He showed me where to push, and we went streaming up to where there were mouse-size animals and a few larger animals.

"These animals were warm-blooded and stayed hidden most of the day, coming out at night," he said. "The dinosaurs would rest at night when it was cold, but the warm-blooded creatures could come out and hunt for food. They ate mostly carrion and insects. A few ate plants, and some ate whatever wasn't moving. We can watch them now because this was using infrared, and we can see as if it were daytime."

"How much video do you have?" I asked.

"Would you believe we actually have hundreds of millions of years of recordings?" Milo said. "Let me show you some more technology." He reached over, opened a small panel, and took out a small bright silver cube about two inches square.

"This is a memory module that has about forty-five thousand years of recording on it. It's a lot like the flash memory humans have recently developed, but it's based on subatomic particle recording. Evolution is so slow that you only need to get close to the time that you are studying. Important things like mass extinctions need closer watching. Let's go take a break and have a snack before we kill off the dinosaurs, all right?"

I agreed. We had been there for several hours, and I hadn't realized I was getting hungry. Besides, I needed to let some of this process move from short-term to long-term memory. I also needed time to think of some things I wanted to ask about. We went to a nearby cafeteria, grabbed a booth, and sat down. I was overwhelmed. "Will we have some time to rest and absorb what I've seen so far?" I asked.

"Of course. I totally understand. It's a lot of stuff in a short period," he replied. "Well, it's Saturday night, so why don't we go out and do something? We can come back to the dinosaurs later."

"Sounds like a plan. Did you say we were going to take a trip later?" I inquired.

"Yeah, something I haven't done in many, many years, and I think you'll enjoy it," he said. "You seem to have a good sense of humor, and this might actually explain some things."

We ate our lunch, which was wonderful, of course.

"Why don't you go to your room and rest while I make preparations for our little adventure? It might be a long night," Milo said. He motioned one of the women over and asked, "Gina, would you mind escorting Mac to his room?"

"It would be my pleasure. Follow me, please," she added.

On the way back, she asked me, "Are you having a good time?"

"I think I am!" I replied.

This was the first female I had encountered up close, and she had all the appearances of being normal. A few normal red-blooded male ideas went fleeting through my head, but they didn't stay long since I still had dinosaur things in there. Boy, did I need a quick catnap. We reached my room, and I thanked her for her assistance. I lay down on the bed for a few minutes and dropped off to sleep, but I woke up in about twenty minutes and felt completely rested.

I turned on the holographic TV and watched the news for a few minutes. There wasn't anything new in the news, but I did notice that whatever channel I went to was in English. I had forgotten about my translators, and I said, "Right ear off." It changed to a Chinese news channel, and they were speaking English and Chinese at the same time. I said, "Left ear off," and I only heard Chinese. I said, "Both ears on," and nothing happened. "Right ear on," I said, and then "Left ear on," and it was back.

Milo knocked on the door, and when I opened it, I saw that he had a garment bag. He handed it to me. "You will need to change into this before we go," he said.

It looked like coveralls, complete with foot coverings and gloves built in. It was tight around the neck and looked sort of bluish gray with no pockets or anything. It looked like some sort of sports gear a luger might wear, but there was no helmet.

"You look great and will easily pass," he said. I had no idea what he was talking about.

"Ready to have some fun?" he asked.

"Sure," I said. "I've never been on a luge."

I thought he would die laughing. "Just wait," he said. "Lugers never had this much fun."

Here we go again, I thought. It reminded me of Monty Python's *And Now for Something Completely Different.*

Chapter Five: Signs

We walked for a while, talking about mostly nothing, until we came to a door that opened into a hangar-like room. There were strange-looking tools on the walls, and what I assumed was test equipment. It could easily be a repair facility, or maybe it was just a hangar. There were four vehicles like the one we'd come down in, except they were a little larger. One of them had its doors open, and a couple of other people were there wearing clothing like ours. We walked over to the craft, and I examined it closely. There were no markings of any kind on it, and it had no windows. It looked like a metallic hockey puck with no rounding on the bottom. It was matte black, and I assumed it was metal. I was wrong, of course. The door was open, but it was not in sight. I figured it opened into the frame, as most of the other doors had.

The bottom of the craft was perfectly flat and a few inches off the floor. In fact, I looked under it and at the others, and they were not touching the floor either. Watching me, Milo asked if I had any questions.

"Only eight to ten million," I replied a bit apprehensively. "What are they sitting on?"

"Nothing. They keep themselves off the floor when their engines are in a resting state. They do have false tripod legs that we extend down when necessary, as you will see later. You thought we didn't have a time machine, but everything seems to be later for you," he laughed. "This is Captain Els and Cocaptain Sandy," Milo said, pointing to each respectively.

They extended their hands, and I shook each of them in turn. Captain Els was tall and thin, as you would expect from most airline pilots. He looked to be around fifty years old by Earth standards, which meant he was probably three hundred plus in reality. Cocaptain Sandy was a bit shorter and appeared to be a little younger.

"We have to have a certified pilot and copilot when we go on a mission with this size craft or larger," Milo said. "Even though they are totally capable of computerized navigation, we still like to have capable Vesi on board in case of a problem. Technology isn't completely without its dangers. We've had a few incidents, so we try to be safe.

"Captains Els and Sandy have checked everything, so we're ready to go," Milo continued. "Even though you don't see any lights on the outside, we have them when we need to make it appear that there are lights and windows. In fact, we can make the outside appear however we want it. We also have sound effects available. Are the signers loaded on?" Milo asked Captain Sandy.

"Sure are—full set. You have your choice of designs tonight," Sandy said with a devilish little smile.

The door closed. We sat down on what looked like extremely comfortable chairs. They appeared to be plastic or fiberglass, and I noticed that mine seemed to mold itself to my rear end and sides. When I sat back and relaxed, the sides and chest area opened slightly and beltlike things went around me from one side to the other and latched. They tightened to the point where I could barely feel them, just like on the smaller craft on which I'd come down here. This was so cool! The whole craft started moving, but there was not a single sound from the engines. The craft went toward the wall, and a portion of the wall opened. We entered a room just slightly larger than the craft and stopped. The wall closed behind us, and water started rushing into the room. In a couple of minutes, it was full. The door opened on the other side, and we entered the Atlantic. It was totally black outside. The only things I could see on any of the windows or screens were a few small lights that I'm sure were from bottom-dwelling creatures. After my eyes adjusted and I looked closer, I saw that there were many all over the place. The few lights from the navigation consoles probably kept me from really seeing everything. I could tell we were moving, but it was difficult to tell in what direction. We seemed to be going more out than up, but who knew.

Milo asked, "Confused?"

I responded, "As usual."

"We are going out into the Atlantic for several miles before we exit the water because we are less likely to be seen. But we want to make a side trip first before we go on our quest," Milo said, looking slyly at the two captains. They just smiled at each other.

After a few minutes, we started to exit the water, and they stopped and checked all the instruments, which I could not read at all because they didn't change to English while I was close. I thought about asking about that but realized there was no reason I would need to know what they said. I could ask if I needed to know anything. So far, everyone had seemed to be open and straightforward with me, if this was for real, that is. We started going up rapidly, and it felt like an express elevator on steroids. I just sat still and went along for the ride.

"Why isn't there any engine noise?" I asked.

"Captains, do you guys want to take this one?" Milo asked.

"Sure," Captain Els replied. "You see, these are gravity engines, or I guess they should be called antigravity engines, so there is no sound, no pollution, and no waste of any kind. They are just repelled by the gravity of the earth and attracted to gravity of other bodies in the universe. Technically, I cannot explain it, but I've had it explained before, and it's too complicated for me to be concerned. Hope that isn't too short of an answer, and I could get one of the transportation specialists to explain it if you'd like.

"I don't think humanity has started seriously working on anything like it yet, so there won't be much information available for you. I can tell you that it has to do with elements that do not exist in enough abundance for detection on Earth or, for that matter, in the galaxy, except in the center parts, where stars are extremely dense and black holes help make these elements. They are similar to elements that your scientists have made. Your scientists are up around element 112 now, but those elements have half-lives of microseconds. If you keep making these elements, there comes a point where they become stable again and are extremely heavy. There is some way to reverse their gravity, and they make great engines if they are controlled."

"Have you ever had an accident with these?" I asked him.

"Only one major one here on Earth. We've lost a few craft on other solar systems due to not knowing all their eccentricities," he went on. "Back in 1908, we lost a ship a little larger than this one. It was hit by some small meteorites on its way back to Earth from a comet inspection out past Pluto. Some sensors were damaged, but we didn't realize it when we started returning into the atmosphere. Incidentally, I keep saying *we* because we normally think of the whole Vesi group as one. I was not on the craft, but I knew the people on board well since it was only about a hundred years ago. Anyway, they came in too fast, and over Siberia instead of the Indian Ocean as they were supposed to. By the time they realized where they were, and the speed they were going, the craft could have caused lots of damage worldwide, so they did a full panic reverse, and the ship exploded in the air just above the forest where they were. We immediately went out there and removed anything we could find that was left. Believe me, there wasn't much. After that, we check all sensors before any reentry, and if problems are found, either they are repaired or another craft is sent to retrieve the crew. We then send the broken craft into the sun for destruction. We've only had to do that once, though.

"We did have a small incident a few years—Earth years—ago, not far from where you live at Vero Beach. It was up the coast at Daytona, and a new pilot was trying his first solo in a small craft like the one you were picked up in. He got distracted by the crowds around the racetrack. He hit the water much too fast, causing a small tsunami, about three or four feet high, at Daytona Beach. Damaged a few cars left parked on the beach, but no humans were hurt. Had he hurt or killed any humans he would never have gotten certified, would you, Sandy?" he said.

Sandy replied, "Yes, it was me, and I love NASCAR, but I'll not fly around there anymore when they are having races. Besides, there are too many weird people there. Any of them could be aliens," he laughed.

"Does that explain it enough for now?" Captain Els asked.

"That's great. I'll try to absorb that," I replied.

Captain Els said, "Humans have a hard time with no engine sound, so I'll turn on some sound effects and you can adjust the pitch and volume here to suit yourself. It will ease your nerves." He pointed to a small joystick, and I heard what sounded like the background noise from *Star Trek*. I adjusted it until it seemed as it should be, knowing that it was not real but still feeling better.

I noticed outside that there was only an occasional light down below. "What altitude are we, what is our speed, and by the way, where the hell are we going?" I inquired.

"We are about forty thousand feet and going about fourteen hundred miles an hour so we don't cause too many sound problems on the surface," Captain Sandy replied. "We are headed east and going over to England before it gets to be daylight over there. In fact, we are rather close and will start descending to our destination." He then turned to Milo. "Have you made your selection yet?"

"No," Milo said excitedly. "Better get on that." Milo got up and touched a small screen. When it came to life, he touched it several times, and pictures of crop circles came up on the screen. He went through several screens and stopped on one that actually looked familiar since I had seen programs on television about them.

"This is one of my favorites," he said. He then moved several parts around, forming a slightly different one, and he touched the screen again. "Done."

"Great," Captain Els said. "Be there in a few minutes."

We were soon over the land, and it looked like daylight was breaking. "What time is it?" I asked.

"About three a.m. local time," Captain Sandy replied. "It just looks like daylight because our sensors can pick up light, heat, or motion and amplify it."

Then we were over a beautiful wheat field without a mark on it—at least that I could see from this height. We went down, and I guessed we were about five hundred to a thousand feet in the air when Captain Els asked Milo if he was ready.

"As they say in the South, 'Let it happen, Cap'n,'" Milo said, touching the screen. In a few seconds, five objects about the size of lawn mowers appeared from under the craft and went down to the wheat field, starting to create the design that Milo had programmed into the screen. They were not lawn mowers because they only bent the grain over instead of cutting it down. They were finished in a matter of minutes. They returned to the ship and stored themselves away.

"I thought there were a couple of men that admitted they did those," I said.

"There have been several humans claiming to have done them, but none of them have been duplicated by anyone, and so the mystery remains," said Milo. "Part of the plan to keep alive the idea that aliens may be making them.

"Due to the time difference, we had to come here first. We are now going to find our guests for the evening back in Georgia," Milo explained. "We have three good ol' boys out on a fishing weekend, and we are going to have them join us for an hour or two so they will report us to the local authorities. It keeps the alien abduction stories alive and at the same time prevents anyone from believing that we truly exist," he went on. "No one gets physically harmed, and they have a story to tell. The tabloids keep the believers believing and the nonbelievers skeptical. Win–win. It's some weird logic by human standards, but it works."

"I guess, but I'm still not sure about this," I said.

"I understand," said Milo. "We've been doing it for centuries on a very limited basis."

I sat back, relaxed, and said to Milo, "I was at the race at Daytona when they had the 'rogue wave,' as they call it. Well, it was actually in the middle of the night, but I'd been on the beach with Karol a few hours before it happened. This was a year or so before she died."

"Yes, I know," said Milo.

"How do you know so much about me?" I asked.

"Since we've got awhile to travel, maybe I can explain some of that," said Milo. "You see, we have video and audio sensors and recorders all over the earth. We've been installing them for millions of years, and they are microscopic and inconspicuous.

"We didn't have many installed in government or military locations until after World War II. We got a surprise at the end of that war. We knew the United States, Germany, and Japan were all working on nuclear energy and nuclear weapons. The thing that surprised us was actually dropping the bomb on inhabited areas. We thought for sure that just a demonstration of the force available would be enough to stop the war. It did stop the war, but that might have also happened if it had been dropped on an uninhabited area, once they witnessed the destruction that was possible.

"When they were dropped bombs on populated cities, we didn't know what to think. After that, we started installing them in all governments and militaries, as well as any other place where life could be studied."

"Could you have prevented it from happening?" I asked.

"No. We are not permitted to interfere with the development of a species," Milo said.

"Not permitted by whom?" I asked.

"Ourselves. We live by our standards, and we can't deviate from them. It has worked for billions of years, and we have no desire to change. We have no crime, no wars, and everything we need for existence, but we are different, as you will find out later, of course.

"The only other time we have been surprised by humans is rock-and-roll music. We weren't expecting that. We thought it was a fad like the music of the nineteen twenties, and what do you know, it's still my favorite music. Speaking of music, how about some? Captain, can we have a little traveling music?" Milo asked.

"Sure," replied Captain Els, touching a panel. Immediately, "Danger Zone" from *Top Gun* began playing, and the pilot started singing along and pretending he was in a dogfight.

"You guys watch too many movies!" Milo laughed.

I sat back, relaxed, closed my eyes for a few minutes, and tried to reassess what I had heard and seen. It wasn't even midnight yet. I couldn't wait until we got to Georgia to see what was in store.

Chapter Six: Abduction

We were coming over land, and I was wondering if I was really up to this, or if maybe the dark side of the Vesi was about to show. The craft slowed, and we were above what looked like a small lake or maybe a reservoir. I saw a campfire to one side. I didn't know it before, but those screens could zoom in on things, and Captain Sandy zoomed one of them down to the campfire. With stunning clarity, we saw three young men sitting around a campfire, laughing and having a good time. We were able to hear what they were saying, as the volume was turned up, and they were arguing about cars. Seems like where there are guys having fun, they'll be talking about cars, women, sports, or complaining about their jobs. These "good ol' boys" seemed to have had an adult beverage or two, for I saw a pickup truck with the bed full of coolers and empty cans. *At least they aren't littering,* I said to myself.

"I'm not sure I feel comfortable with this," I said to Milo. "These are people, after all, and I feel a connection whether I know them or not."

"Let me explain a little about this," said Milo. "This is not a random event. It has been in the planning for a while, but we've been waiting for the right opportunity. We hardly ever do anything that is unplanned. These gentlemen are local people, and we know all about them. The one wearing the Braves T-shirt is John Bob. The one in the "Wishin' I was fishin'" T-shirt is George Bob, and the other person is Bob Bob. You know all Southerners have Bob as a middle name." Milo winked and smiled at his little joke.

"For real, the Braves guy is Jonathon Jackson Jones," he said. "He sells building supplies to contractors and goes by the nickname 'J-Three.' The gentleman in the fishin' T-shirt is a small-time contractor named George Wilkerson, and he's usually called GW. The other one is Robert Owens, who does go by Bob, and he is a loan officer at a small bank. They all do business with each other and pal around on weekends sometimes. They are all above average in intelligence and well suited for this mission. Although they do not know they have been included in it, I can assure there will be no harm done to them."

J-Three had a beard and mustache and was stoutly built. GW had a mustache and a short ponytail and was thin but strongly built. Bob was clean-shaven and could have probably passed for a policeman. He had a short crew cut and looked as if he was probably right out of the military. They all looked like they were in their late twenties or early thirties. I could find out from Milo if it was important, but it certainly wasn't just then. I was more concerned for their safety.

"I do feel better, but I'm still a little apprehensive," I said.

"As well you should be," replied Milo. "Let's watch and listen in a little."

"Ford stands for first on race day," J-Three said.

"You're mostly right. It actually stands for *failure* on race day," GW said with a laugh.

"Chevrolet was named after a Frenchman," J-Three replied. "They always stop with their wheels in the air when they see the white flag."

"You're both wrong," Bob said. "Dodge is named that because they have to dodge the Ford and Chevy parts that fall off all over the track."

"Dodge!" J-Three replied. "Chrysler products are only driven by old farts. The driver has to stop every five laps to try to pee."

"Besides, they have to put a left turn signal on the car so it can stay on the whole race," added GW.

"Anyone else need one?" Bob called as he walked over to the truck and opened a cooler. He took out a fresh Bud Light.

"Me too," both of the others replied, tossing their empties in the pickup bed.

Bob opened the other coolers and retrieved a Miller Lite and an Old Milwaukee for the others. I could see they had different opinions about beer also.

Captain Els said it was time to get the craft ready for the mission.

Mission? I wondered if this was anything like the mission they had in mind for me.

He pressed a spot on the panel and said, "Lights on, tripod feet extended, external engine noise, port holes, communications jammed. I think we are ready. Time to suit up."

He opened a panel and took out some alien head covers somewhat like the ones they had on when I first arrived. The heads were larger, with almond-shaped shiny black eyes, and were gray to match the rest of our suit. Each had a small slit for a mouth, two holes for a nose, and a hole on each side for an ear. When I put it on, I was surprised at how well I was able to see and hear. It was some type of material that allowed a person to see out, but others couldn't see in—like the material people put on their car windows.

Milo said, "You will understand what we say, but they will only understand us when we speak English, which will be very limited."

The pilot made a slow pass over the lake, right in front of the guys, and then slowed down and came to a complete stop. The outside of the craft now had what looked like lights and portholes on it. I told myself that I had to remember to ask how they do that. He was allowing them to see us, and for a moment, they said nothing.

Then J-Three noticed us and said, "Do you see that! There's a damn flying saucer!"

"I see it!" Bob and GW exclaimed almost at the same time.

"We got to report this to the sheriff!" Bob said. By this time, they were all standing and pointing as GW reached and picked up a cell phone.

"Totally dead!" he said.

"Mine too," both Bob and J-Three added after they had opened their phones.

"What the hell we gonna do now?" GW asked.

"I'm not driving!" Bob proclaimed. "As much as we've been drinking, we walk into the sheriff's office, we won't walk out. Sheriff Blake can be a prick when he wants, and he usually wants."

"It's coming this way!" J-Three screamed as we slowly slid over the top of them. A bright light from under the craft bathed the entire area around them, including the pickup, in light. The light scanned around as if it were searching for something and then directed itself to a wide spot in the dirt road out behind their pickup. We slowly descended, and the craft settled on the tripod feet that we had extended. They were about three feet across and made an impression in the dirt about three or four inches deep. Some dust kicked up into the air.

"Just for effect," Captain Els commented. The engine sounds slowly decreased until there was just a sort of *ping* coming from the craft. "The UFOers love that sound," the captain added.

The guys were just standing there, looking and not saying a single word. Their eyes looked like saucers, no pun intended. They looked as if they were hypnotized. If it had not been during a warm part of the year, you could have sworn they were frozen—just staring at the craft. The door to the craft appeared, and steps lowered to the ground.

"Just follow along," Milo said. As the others exited, I fell into line, and we all got out and just stood there for a few seconds. Then they started walking toward the guys, and I wondered if they would start to run.

"Don't be afraid," Milo said. "We are not here to harm you. We are friendly. We would just like to interview you. Would you please come with us?"

The three started walking slowly toward us as if in a trance. They followed Captain Els into the ship, with us following them. He took them individually to three different small rooms on the ship and pointed to a chair for each.

The rooms looked a lot like a normal doctor's exam rooms, with a table, a couple of chairs, and various instruments on the walls and surrounding counters. There was a slight hint of medicine, or probably just antiseptic, in the air. The doors were all closed, and we waited a few moments before going back to the control room. Milo opened a compartment and took out a new head cover, which had bright red hair and bright green eyes. A reddish cast slowly started at the neck. Otherwise, the head was like the ones we wore.

"Music on," he said, and we started walking down to the first room.

Captain Els went in first and said, "The doctor wants to check you out. Would you please get on the table here and put this over your mouth and nose?" J-Three got on the table just as he was told, and he put the mask on. Milo came into the room and bent over J-Three, whose eyes were so fixed on the doctor that I thought they would dry out. I noticed that Bach classical music was playing loud enough to hear in the background.

Milo said, "I'm just going to examine you a little." J-Three closed his eyes and fell asleep. Milo and Captain Els then took off the mask and started to strip the clothes off J-Three. I didn't know what was going to happen, but Milo had assured me they would not be harmed. They stripped J-Three down to his underwear and put his clothes in an opening in the wall. I didn't understand what was going on, but no one seemed to have been hurt.

Milo then came over with a small instrument, put it over the mouth of J-Three, and said, "Great." I saw the number: .024 percent. Milo then went into the control room and came out this time with a different head on. It had bright green hair, yellow eyes, and a greenish tint.

We went into the next room, where Bob was already on the table. The background music was country and western. The same thing was repeated, but this time the reading was .019 percent. Bob's boxers had Burger King logos all over them, which read, "Home of the Whopper." Guess the guy was a bragger. We didn't check to find out since it didn't seem to be part of the mission.

Then Milo changed to a head with yellow hair and bright blue eyes. We entered the room with GW in it, and there was rap music playing in the background. Everything went just as before, except the reading was .020 percent and his shorts had been taken off and put on backward.

I asked what the reading was and Milo said, "Blood alcohol. We needed good readings for this mission."

"Want a beer?" Milo asked.

"Sure," I responded, following all the Vesi out of the craft. I noticed that the outside of the craft was now flat black again.

"Just in case we might have prying eyes, but last we checked, no one was within several miles of here, although there are a couple of deer and a possum or two wondering what is going on," Captain Sandy said with a laugh. "Anyway, if humans get closer than a couple of miles, we will be notified by the ship. We will have ample time to get scarce."

We walked over to the pickup and got a beer each. Everyone took off their head covers. I looked at the two captains, and Milo noticed.

"It's okay. We're only having one, and besides, the pilots used to work for Northwest. They're used to it." He laughed, as did the captains and I. We chitchatted about the lake and what a great spot it was for a weekend fishing trip, and for a moment, I forgot the three aliens were several hundred years old and from a vaporized solar system, living almost thirty thousand feet underwater. I realized that intelligent beings might be pretty much the same universe-wide, and then I thought that maybe humans aren't intelligent just yet, but that we had potential. We were having fun just like the good ol' boys were before we arrived, and I wondered what their fate was.

"How long will they be out?" I asked.

"About an hour and a half," Milo said. "It's almost time to go." Everyone got up, and Milo, Els, and Sandy took the coolers out of the pickup bed. They opened them and started opening and pouring the beers out on the ground, putting the empty cans in a garbage bag. There was about a case in each of the coolers, and it took several minutes to empty them all.

"Why are you doing that?" I asked.

"Part of the mission script," Milo said. "You'll see as things develop."

"Later?" I asked.

"Later," Milo laughed.

We loaded a cooler and some empty cans into the same place the clothes had gone earlier, and then we returned our fake heads to the storage area. We started the craft upward and stopped about a hundred feet off the ground. Captain Sandy pushed a place on the control panel screen, and out from under the craft came those little things that had made the crop circles. They proceeded to where the tripod tracks were in the dirt road. They settled over them, one over each, and dust came up around them. In about thirty seconds, they returned to the craft and disappeared underneath. The dust clouds blew away, and I saw that the tracks were gone; the ground looked as if nothing had ever been there. There were even tire tracks as there had been before.

We slowly made our way just above the treetops and toward the small town that was a few miles away. We followed the dirt road until it connected with a paved road, and then we followed that. Along the way, articles of clothes were dropped at random, along with empty beer cans. By the time we reached the town, almost all the cans and clothing had been scattered like a trail. When we got close to the city, I saw that there was a small park with a wide open area in the middle for playing games. We landed there. About ten of the empty cans and the cooler were deposited in a pile close to the picnic tables. The men's shoes and socks were put in a pile.

We returned to the ship, and Milo and each captain went into the rooms and put a small mask over each one of the guys and then took it off to revive them. The guys moved around, and each one was told to come along. They followed like zombies, walking out of the ship with assistance from the Vesi. They were led to the picnic tables and told to sit down. An empty can was placed in each of their hands, and they were told to lay their heads down for a nap, which they did. We got back into the ship, rose up several hundred feet into the dark, and stopped. We watched and listened on the screens, and in a couple of minutes, the guys woke up as if they had indeed napped, looking at each other dumbfounded.

"Where in the hell are we?" GW asked. "Where are our clothes?"

"We're in the county park," Bob said, looking around. "The sheriff's office is about a quarter of a mile from here."

They found their shoes and socks and put them on, and Bob noticed that his underwear was on backward.

"Oh my God," he said. "What did they do to us?"

They walked rapidly to the sheriff's office, barging in excitedly, and said loudly, "We were abducted by a UFO!"

The deputy looked them up and down and asked, "Who was the pilot, Jim Beam or Jack Daniels?"

"Really!" Bob said. "We can show you. We were at the lake, and they picked us up and made us go with them. They dropped us at the park."

"Right," said the deputy. "I'd better call Sheriff Blake. I don't think he's going to be happy."

He went to the phone, and we only heard the deputy's side of the conversation. "Sorry to wake you, Sheriff, but we got three of the locals in, and they are almost naked and said they were abducted from the lake and dropped at the park." Pause. "Yes, it smells and looks like they were, but they walked in." Pause. "No, I didn't see any of them driving, and there is no car out front." Pause. "Okay, about twenty, and I'll test them while you're on the way. Later, Chief." He hung up the phone.

"Okay, gentlemen, I need you to blow into these for me while the chief is coming down." He handed each one a Breathalyzer and jotted down the readings. "I sure hope you guys didn't drive here," he said.

"We didn't," J-Three said. "We walked from the park, where we were dropped off."

"Guess those aliens can't read the sign that says the park closes at dark," the deputy said. All this time, the dispatcher was giggling in the background.

"Why did they keep your clothes? Hope none of y'all got pregnant. Those children sure would be ugly," the dispatcher added.

"Now, just leave these boys alone," said the deputy. "We have to investigate this like real police officers. Everybody is innocent until proven guilty. The sheriff is here; he'll handle this."

The sheriff walked into the station, stopped, and looked at the whole situation for a minute. He walked over to the deputy and said, "Got the test results?"

"Yep, as you suspected, over the limit. But like I said, there is no proof they did any driving, and there haven't been any complaints tonight against them."

The sheriff sat them down and started asking them questions. They all tried to talk at once.

"Tell you what, why don't we go into my office one at a time and let me get the stories from each of you," the sheriff said.

One by one, they went into the sheriff's office and repeated their stories. They were almost identical, except the part about the doctor. The hair, eyes, and music playing were all different. The sheriff seemed not to believe them, saying, "Why don't we take a little ride and see what's going on?"

"We'll show you where they dropped us off … and where their spacecraft landed and the marks it made," GW said.

They all got into the sheriff's car along with the deputy. They drove to the park, and the deputy got out and unlocked the gate across the road, pushing it back. He drove over by the picnic tables and found the coolers and empty cans. He gave them all a good hard stare.

"Boys, you know the park is closed at night, and there is no alcohol allowed anytime. Not counting the littering," said the sheriff.

"I swear we didn't do this! Those things must have done it!" Bob said.

"Let's go look at the lake and see what's there," said the sheriff, getting back into the car. They drove through the park gate, and the sheriff stopped to let the deputy get out and relock the gate. They started going back up the road and turning toward the lake. He stopped almost immediately.

"What's that beside the road?" said the sheriff. He turned toward the deputy and pointed at something at the edge of the headlights.

"Let me see," said the deputy. He exited the car and slowly walked over and picked up a pair of pants, holding them up in the headlights. He also picked up a couple of empties.

"Bring 'em here," said the sheriff. The deputy returned to the car and held them up to the guys in the backseat.

"Belong to any of you?" the deputy asked as he reached into the back pocket and pulled out a wallet. "Mr. Wilkerson, I think these are yours, according to your license."

He handed them to GW, who opened his wallet and started going through it. "I don't see anything missing," he said.

The deputy drove a little farther and stopped again, this time turning his spotlight on the roadside. "Whose shirt?" he asked.

The guys looked, and Bob said "Hey, wait, that's my shirt! What's going on here?"

"Damn good question," said the sheriff. The deputy retrieved the shirt and handed it to Bob. The sheriff slowly drove down the road with his spotlight on the shoulder. He occasionally stopped, and the deputy got out and retrieved an article of clothing. This continued all the way to the lake, and by the time they arrived, all three guys had their clothes back on.

"Stop!" said J-Three.

The sheriff stopped and looked around.

"Right up ahead is where the UFO landed. You'll see the marks it made. It was real heavy."

The sheriff put his high beams on and turned his spotlight on the road. Everyone slowly got out of the car. "Right where?" the sheriff asked.

"Right here," said J-Three, pointing to the ground around him.

"Were they driving?" the sheriff asked. "I only see tire tracks around here. Get back in the car. I think you boys need a good rest."

"I swear we're telling the truth! We were abducted for about two hours and woke up in the park," they were all saying excitedly. "Why would we make this up?"

"From all the cans and clothes we found, I don't have any idea what went on and I don't think I want to know." The sheriff went on, "Wait a minute. Let me think." The sheriff paused for a few seconds and said, "If I take y'all in, I'll have to fill out reports for hours, and since y'all don't seem to have caused any problems with anyone except whoever has to clean up the cans, I have an idea. If I let you guys sleep here for the night, will you not drive? In fact, I'll take the pickup keys back to the office. When you guys wake up and are sober, call the office and someone will bring the keys out to you. How does that sound? Besides, there's no proof anything happened, so we'll just let this be our little secret."

"Unless you all turn up pregnant with alien babies," laughed the deputy.

"Cut that out, Clifford," said the sheriff. "We have to see if there are any other reports of UFOs tonight." It was clear that it was all he could do to keep from laughing.

The sheriff checked to make sure there was no beer available, and once he was satisfied, he held out his hand and said, "Keys. Oh, and check your cell phones to make sure they're working. You said they were dead earlier."

They all checked, and all of them were working. They looked at each other as if they thought that maybe they'd just been drunk.

"I'll be seeing you boys after you get well, if you know what I mean," said the sheriff. He and the deputy got in the cruiser and drove off.

"Let's just get some sleep, and I don't think I'll say a word to the wife," said Bob. The other two agreed but said they might call the tabloids and see if the story was worth beer money later on. With that, they got their sleeping bags out of the pickup and curled up around the campfire.

We all sat back and were strapped in. We headed back while it was still dark, slowly entering the Atlantic to get back home.

Home, I thought. I was starting to believe I was part of this, and then I thought that might not be a bad thing. I was going to have my little inferior human brain working overtime for a while. When we got back, Captains Els and Sandy said they enjoyed my company, and Captain Els said maybe he would see me on a future trip.

Surprised, I looked at Milo, and he smiled and said, "Later. Let's get some rest. Tomorrow we have to find out what happened to the dinosaurs." I had almost forgotten about them. He walked me to my room and said, "See you when you are rested."

"Good night," I said. I went into the room and lay directly down on the bed. My mind was still going a thousand miles an hour when I finally drifted off to sleep.

Chapter Seven: Killing the Dinosaurs

I woke up and realized I still had my clothes on. I remember that I was still processing what happened last night as I went to sleep. I felt better now after I replayed the abduction, and I wondered how many of the stories you heard were like this one. I started some coffee, undressed, and took a shower. Again, there were fresh clothes in the closet. I put them on. By this time, the coffee was ready, and I noticed a small refrigerator in the kitchen. I looked inside, and it had all kinds of drinks and snacks, all of which I liked. I figured they must have been spying on me for a while. I reminded myself to ask about it … *later*.

I had some orange juice and coffee and looked over the Sunday paper. No abduction stories or anything weird in the paper. Then there was a knock on the door. I went and opened it, and there was Milo smiling.

"Ready to go kill the dinosaurs?" he asked.

"Sure," I replied. "This is something we humans have been arguing about since the first one was discovered."

"And you have been mostly correct," Milo said.

"Later?" I asked.

"Yep," he said. We started walking, and Milo said, "You're probably wondering how we know so much about you, aren't you, Mac?"

"I just figured I had been bugged, but I don't know why you would be interested in showing and telling me all this stuff," I said.

"We actually have a mission that includes you, and I will explain fully in the coming week. We will not have enough time this weekend to show you everything that you need to know, so I'll be seeing you topside this week, and we'll have a few discussions before the trip we have planned for you. That trip includes the moon and Mars. You will understand after you see some of our technologies later today. I need you to understand why you were selected for this mission, and as trivial as it may seem, it may be important for the future of the humans and the Vesi. Remember that we are in for the long haul and can't influence human development. This is going to be a slight exception, and we have done this very few times throughout human history. More on that later," he added.

By this time, we were back at the theater where Milo had shown me the other holographs of the dinosaurs. We went in, and there was already a scene going on. Dinosaurs were busy doing dinosaur things, and the smell was musty and it felt humid. We walked through the forest and sat down at the console in the middle of an opening in the forest. I had fun running my hand through bushes and trees on the way. There was no sensation of texture as I went through them. They sure looked real, though. This wasn't a small room, but the projection looked as if we were outside, complete with sky. The only difference I could easily tell was that the floor was flat instead of having a more natural feel. I think the smell and sound enhanced the whole experience. I then got one of those human ideas about how much money I could make with one of these. With just the technology I had seen so far, I could make Bill Gates look like a commoner. Then I stopped myself. Maybe I should pay attention.

"Is there any time period you would like to go to before we kill these great creatures?" Milo asked.

"I would just like to look around for awhile. Would that be possible?" I replied.

"I thought you might like to, so I'm going to show you how to use the projector more in depth, and you can go to any time period you like," Milo said. "The only restriction is that I would like to be here for the end, so I am excluding that cube until I return. I am going to go make some arrangements for this afternoon, and I will leave you here for a couple of hours to look around. Let me show you how."

I'd had some experience with it already, but Milo showed me more detailed instructions on how to use the joystick. He also showed me how I could fast-forward either where I was in a scene or in time. I could sit at one place and fast-forward or reverse it and watch evolution of the earth and the creatures. There was an infinitely variable method for changing the speed of time, and I thought this was the most exciting thing I had ever seen. Boy, I would have loved to bring my class and show them this, but I knew that would not be possible.

Milo said I had access to almost any time in the history of the earth—and from many different places. The only time period currently loaded in the projector was the one with the dinosaurs, from the time they were just starting to rule the earth until they were exterminated. From the way he said "exterminated," I thought for a moment that it might have been deliberate. But I didn't think the Vesi would do anything like that. Milo turned on a panel, and English appeared. There was a time scale in English, and he showed me how to zoom in on a particular era, down to the date and even the time of the day if I wanted to go that close.

The time scale started around five hundred million years ago, and I noticed that it currently had the days lasting 20.05 hours. When I moved the joystick, the closer it was to the current time, the longer the days were. The earth had been slowing down since its creation. Just think: someday a day might be 8,700 hundred hours long. If the earth lasted long enough, it would end up just like the moon, which doesn't spin in relation to the earth and shows the same face to us all the time. The earth would not spin in relation to the sun. That wouldn't be good for anybody. I wasn't worried because I was sure that I (and everything else) would be long gone. It was the first time I truly understood why the moon only shows one side. It could be microscopically rotating, but we haven't been observing it long enough to notice. Maybe someday they would put a laser there and find the microscopic rotation in relation to the earth. That's how they found out the moon is receding from the earth about an inch and half a year.

I was getting excited. There was a place where, from what looked like a space station or something, I could get a view of the earth. I could watch the earth take shape from when there was only one continent called Pangaea, around two to three hundred million years ago. I could watch the drift of the continents and the changing icecaps and everything. This could put all the paleontologists, geologists, and half the rest of the scientific community out of their jobs. I wondered what all there was to learn from the Vesi. I played with the viewer excitedly for a while and lost track of time.

When Milo returned, I looked up, surprised that it had been over two hours. I felt as if I'd just skimmed the surface. It was much like when the Internet first started and there were so many things to look for. Then I realized I had not had a single pop-up ad or any e-mails offering to mortgage my house or enlarge my penis. If humans had access to this, nothing would ever get done again, I'm sure. People would just sit and go through history, saying, "I knew that's how it happened" and "Would you look at this!"

Milo saw my excitement and said that once things were finalized with the mission I could come and play all I wanted. I was so thrilled. And to think that talking to a dolphin was impressive yesterday. I was so scared I would wake up and find that the whole thing was the result of getting a bad bowl of chili from Denny's.

"Do you want to kill the dinosaurs or have lunch first?" Milo asked.

"Let's exterminate them first, or I'll be too excited to eat," I said.

"Okay, let me bring in the cubes that have that time on them," Milo said. He pressed some places that I could not read on the console. A new scene soon appeared, and I noticed a new time scale in the sixty-five-million-year-ago range. "We'll go slowly, and we are going to go to a place that would have been in southern Mexico at the present time. The continents were a little different than they are today."

"So we're right about the asteroid?" I asked.

"Mostly," Milo said. "We were aware of the incoming asteroid. We had tracked it and knew it was going to impact, but we were not permitted to prevent it. It was about nine and a half miles in average diameter because it was, of course, not round; it looked more like a tumbling potato. It was traveling at roughly twenty-five thousand miles per hour, or eleven kilometers per second. This is what you refer to as hauling ass.

"We knew there would be a big problem for everything," he continued. "So we uploaded most of the data we had saved to a ship away from Earth, and we took all our ships off the earth to watch from a distance. Remember that at this time, we lived on the surface in sturdy buildings that were mostly metal and stonelike material. Occasionally, one of us would get caught by a creature, and they seemed to like our type. Guess we were warm compared to the reptiles they normally feasted on. The mammals were tiny and quick at that time, and they stayed hidden during most of the daytime.

"Watch while I go slowly up to the point of impact, and you can see the meteorite coming in. The atmosphere isn't that thick when you are traveling at that speed, but you'll still see the fireball form. The atmosphere is about a thousand kilometers thick, but most of it is in the lowest eleven kilometers. The meteorite took only one second to go through that since it came in almost straight. Watch closely. Here it comes," he said. There was a brilliant flash and a feeling of intense heat for a second. Then everything disappeared from the scene. The theater had no scene at all.

"What happened?" I asked.

"Those cameras and sensors were vaporized by the meteorite. Lots of others were still working for a while, and we will look at some of those," Milo explained.

Milo pressed some other places on the console. A scene appeared, and we were somewhere else, the feeling of heat suddenly engulfing us. There were fires breaking out all over the place, but it wasn't totally in flames as I had thought it might be. There was smoke and dust raising everywhere, and the dinosaurs seemed to stop and look at what was happening. They weren't all roasted, as some scientists would say, but it was definitely very warm and growing dark from all the debris in the air. The EPA would have been pissed had they been here. Milo fast-forwarded these scenes, and some dinosaurs seemed to be dying for no real apparent reason other than there was just too little to eat since things were going extinct quite rapidly. There was a drastic change in the climate, and it got extremely cold. I needed a jacket.

"There are still some dinosaurs here, as you can see, but there isn't much food. Notice anything about the remaining dinosaurs?" Milo asked.

I looked closely, unable to detect anything at first. All of a sudden, I noticed. "They're all males!"

"Correctamundo," said Milo. "Not enough females available worldwide to keep things going, along with all the other things that happened. I thought you might be interested since you teach biology. In the cold-blooded reptiles, the temperature largely determines sex. Also in mammals to some extent, but since the determination in mammals is inside the body, it is pretty close to fifty-fifty. In the reptiles, the environment around the incubating eggs mostly determines the sex. Of course, you know that."

He continued, "And why did the alligators survive pretty much unchanged? Where do they mostly live? In the water that wasn't affected as much as the land. They built their nests close to the water, and you will notice that during this time, they were mostly in the water. The bird ancestors were warm-blooded and were able to sustain the species because environmental temperatures weren't as big a factor as in the other cold-blooded reptiles. Notice also that the mammals prevailed and started to come out in the daylight since there were so few dinosaurs and they weren't in very good shape. The mammals had a rough time, but being warm-blooded prevented their extinction. A few reptiles survived, but they were mostly water dwellers, and the water was not affected as much as the air was. Some of the smaller warm-blooded dinos survived because they were warm-blooded, and they evolved into modern-day birds. Snakes and a few other reptiles live underground most of the time. Most species went extinct. Seventy to ninety percent, we estimate. Now, are you ready to go and get a bite of one of the descendents of the creatures you just saw?"

"Am I ever!" I said, while trying to take a mental inventory of all the things I had just seen. I couldn't wait to get some stick time on that console. Except for Ralph and Hide and Seek, I didn't really want to go home. I knew I would never again be able to look at a piece of fried chicken without thinking about the dinosaurs. Milo turned the console off, and we headed to the nearest cafeteria. I couldn't bring myself to get the chicken. I had seen their original fried ancestor. A mammal didn't sound good right then either, so I selected a salad with shrimp since I didn't think I'd seen any of their relatives today.

As we ate, we chitchatted about pets. I found out that no pets were allowed down here, but the Vesi on the surface were allowed to have them as long as they weren't exotic, which would make them stand out. Most of them picked dogs and cats, but a few had fish and some even had reptiles.

After lunch, Milo said we would take a break for an hour or two before we got started in the afternoon. It might be a late night, and we had many technologies to cover quickly. I went to my room and immediately dropped off to sleep as soon as I lay down. I was exhausted. After all, I had just exterminated 90 percent of life on Earth … and it was barely afternoon.

Chapter Eight: Technology

Milo woke me, and off we went. We started walking, and he told me that I would likely see some new things that humans would probably invent someday. He said that he didn't fully understand some of the stuff himself, but he would try his best to explain when he could. We went into a huge room, about the size of an aircraft hangar, which was stacked floor to ceiling with what looked like some kind of storage racks. These were filled with cubical boxes, and Milo went over and picked out one of the boxes, placing it on the floor. He opened it by tilting the top back, and inside were smaller cubes. He took one of those out and tilted the top back on it. Inside this were smaller cubes in a ten-by-ten configuration. He said it was a compact flash memory module that used single photons for bits. One of those could probably hold all the data we had in all the libraries on Earth.

"What would happen if there was a disaster of some kind here?" I asked.

"There are backup copies on two other planets, and they have backups here and at other sites," Milo replied. "This is just one of the sites here on Earth, and data is continually being backed up and sent to each other. We also have an extensive DNA library of almost every creature that ever lived on the earth. Maybe someday the dinosaurs will return if we need a real adventure game." He laughed.

Milo put the cube back, and we left and walked down a hallway for another few minutes, coming to what looked like a laboratory of some kind. There weren't all the flasks and glassware that you would expect in a lab. Instead, there were more instruments, and several Vesi were busy with their heads down under hoods. You could see that they were watching either flat screens or holographic projectors while doing their various things. They didn't seem to notice our arrival and continued working on whatever they were doing.

Milo said, "Let's start with the basics and work our way up. We need to go look at the atom itself, and then maybe some of the other stuff will make more sense."

He motioned for me to follow him, and we moved over to a machine, which he turned on. There was a holographic projection of the universe. "This is a reproduction, not the actual universe. It is used for demonstration, and we can zoom in," he said. He then started to zoom slowly in on a galaxy and then a solar system, then a planet, a continent, tree, leaf, cell, nucleus, DNA molecule, atom, and electron. I had seen something like this on the Internet before, but they stopped at the molecular level.

He stopped and said, "That's where most humans go to, and even that isn't exactly clear. Watch this." He then zoomed into the electron, and it looked like a small solar system, but things were more uniform and the particles were circulating in different planes. I had never seen anything like it. I was staring at what was a completely new world, at least to me.

"These are quark-like particles and they are made of smaller particles ... and we are now down to photons. Here is where it gets interesting," he said. "Look at the photon." It looked like an elliptical orbit that was everywhere at once. It slowed down. He pressed a control, and I could see that it was orbiting and changing its orbit slightly. Then it came to a halt slowly, and I noticed that it was elliptical and was changing from a horizontal to a vertical configuration as if it were tumbling.

He then put what looked like a light beam on the viewer and said, "This is a single beam of light that would not even be visible to the naked eye." It started slowing down, and I could see that it was photons like I had just seen, but they were connected into what looked like a chain, with every other link being horizontal and the ones in between vertical.

"This is why they act like both particles and waves—they are," said Milo. "Also, we've discovered that there are as many smaller levels as there are larger levels. Our universe may all be part of a pimple on a yak's butt in a larger universe," he added. "We have been studying the string theory and have determined it might be better to call it the chain theory. We're kind of stuck in this universe because the smaller ones are so hard to see and work with, and the larger ones are so vast. This one we're living in isn't too bad, though."

"I'm starting to understand a few things better," I said.

"Now you're starting to see things from a Vesi point of view," Milo said.

"Why don't you let all humans in on this stuff?"

"In time, if they ever become civilized, they will discover this," Milo said.

"Civilized? I thought we were pretty civilized."

"We will discuss that in detail later this week, and I'll explain our position," Milo said.

Milo adjusted the viewer, and other particles appeared. "Now," he said, "I want to try to explain what we have found on dark matter and dark energy. I'll try to explain this in terms that I'm sure you will be able to understand. To the best of our knowledge, nothing actually exists." He paused to wait for a reaction. I just sort of stared and thought about that. "It's all just various forms of energy, and the net result is zero." He paused to let this sink in. "There are so many miniscule things in the atom, and we are still discovering new things all the time. Everything seems to be made of something smaller—and vice versa."

I was still trying to get a grasp on this. Just how many things were in the atom was still a question that science was trying to answer. I was having another "human moment," thinking how many Nobel Prizes I could win and how popular I would be, but to my surprise, it went away quickly enough to make me proud of myself.

"The universe is said to be devoid of matter except what is visible, but just the opposite seems to be the case," Milo went on. "The universe is totally full of particles, or I should say pieces of energy, smaller than neutrinos. It's as if we're swimming in this stuff that we can't see, feel, taste, or, for that matter, even detect. These particles may even be made of something smaller. The Vesi call these 'Flynn particles.'" Milo waited for a few seconds.

"Is that the name of the person that discovered them or conceived them?" I asked.

"No, the Vesi that came up with the concept was watching an old Errol Flynn movie when it popped into her head," Milo replied. "As far as we are concerned, there is no such thing as vacant space. These particles are what allow us to contact each other at speeds almost instantaneously … and for gravity to be able to know about every other particle in the known universe.

"Here is the strange part of dark matter and dark energy. As near as we can figure, dark energy and dark matter are the same. Dark energy is kind of like the liquid version of dark matter. The real exciting part has to do with black holes. Visible matter, including light, is sucked into black holes. This we know—and humans assume. The thing you don't know is that in there, this visible matter is converted to dark matter and is expelled back out. That is why the closer you get to the center of galaxies, the more of it there is."

Milo paused for me to catch up. I thought about this for a few seconds and could come up with no argument.

"This is also the reason that the outer stars of galaxies rotate around the center at the same speed as the inner stars. All the stars in the galaxy are in a sort of dark matter/dark energy gel. This increase in dark matter is also causing the universe to expand instead of contract, as it should be doing by the force of gravity. Dark matter is packed shoulder-to-shoulder, if you know what I mean."

"Hang on a second till I get my head around this," I said. "Would this be like taking a balloon full of water and, oh, let's say buttons, and having them float around in there for my universe?"

"Okay, but let's make this *thick* water so these buttons, the galaxies, stay sorta in place," said Milo.

"Good. Now I would put some seltzer tablets all around this mixture, and they would change and expand, causing the balloon, my universe, to expand instead of contract as the elastic, my gravity, in my balloon is trying to do."

"Correctamundo again." Milo smiled with approval. "You get a ninety-nine percent for today's quiz."

"Why not one hundred percent?" I asked.

"No theory is absolutely perfect," he laughed. "Besides, we'll probably use a curve."

"I'll accept that."

Milo continued. "We have not been able to find an end or edge to the universe, but we have had some strange things happen, like sending robot sensors to the edge and having them return from the other direction with their sensors totally confused. One of the problems is that we are restricted to the speed of light in our sensors and our minds, but we know that is not the limit. The speed of light is like the flat Earth concept we all had at one time. The universe expanded at many times the speed of light right after the Big Bang. It may be a limit when particles are big enough to be detected by anything we can make, but we know it isn't the limit for the rest of the universe. See why it's a lot easier just to say a higher power made it … and that's good enough? We have no proof that that isn't true either way." He studied me closely. "Do you need a break before we continue?"

"Definitely," I answered. "I think I blew out a few brain cells."

We went and had a coffee, just chatting about nonscientific items and letting our brains cool for a few minutes.

"There are lots more things we need to show you and discuss with you, but some of it will have to wait until later this week," said Milo.

"Remember, I need to be in school tomorrow," I said.

"Yes, and you will be. You need to go home and think about everything. When I visit you later this week, we'll have some deep discussions about next weekend's trips to make sure you would like to go," Milo said. "You need a couple of days to try to absorb this weekend and then to determine what questions you may have about the Vesi and other things. I'm sure there has been a lot of confusion. We have scratched the surface of many subjects. You need to review your adventures so far, and I'm sure you will come up with more questions than answers.

"There's at least one more area I would like to show you, and maybe it will answer a few things," Milo said. "We'll go through some of these atomic things sometime, spending some time answering how we discovered the subatomics."

We left that lab and walked down a hallway until we reached another lab. When I got in range of it, the sign changed to read Biology Lab 7. We walked in to find many people working at the hooded consoles, just as before, and they were working on or observing cells, organisms, and so forth. I happened to look at one of the consoles, seeing what looked like a red blood cell, but it was about the size of a basketball. Everything was so easy to see. The Vesi was taking apart a mitochondrion organelle and zooming in on parts of it, even down to the atomic level.

"I'm going to show you something that will explain a couple of things that were in the later bucket," Milo said. He then turned on a console and started a holographic projection of a DNA molecule.

"Recognize this?" he asked.

"Yep, good ol' DNA. The famous double helix," I said.

"Correctamundo again," Milo said. "Human DNA is a double helix and only made of four amino acids. These are adenine, thymine, cytosine, and guanine. Now here is Vesi DNA, or the equivalent. Notice anything different?"

"I sure do," I said. There was a helix all right, but it was a quad helix, and there were a couple of amino acids I did not recognize. "What are those?" I asked.

"Those are a couple of right-handed amino acids not naturally found on Earth. All amino acids used by humans are left-handed ones, as you know. This is one of the reasons there is no interbreeding between the humans and Vesi. The right-handed ones enable the helix to be quad instead of double. We take supplements that we make here and on several other systems also. Human bodies would just ignore them."

Milo adjusted the viewer to show a close up of the molecule. He continued, "Our DNA has a sort of backup test, and it's one of the reasons we have a limited problem with diseases. Again, we also reproduce a little bit differently, and I'll discuss that later. Also, our DNA doesn't shorten each time it duplicates, and we end up living longer since there is no DNA wear out. The Vesi DNA doesn't duplicate in two opposite directions and end up with a problem with the telomeres as human DNA does. We wear out and die from other reasons, but we do live much longer."

The viewer was adjusted to illustrate the DNA replication. We watched for a little while.

"We can still have accidents and occasionally do. Topside, we occasionally lose a member. If you did a DNA test on a Vesi, it would just read inconclusive since the right-handed amino acids would not be reproduced. No one will ever be able to tell unless he does X-ray images of it, and there is no reason to do that. Just in case, when a Vesi is killed accidentally, we sometimes have to retrieve the body to keep any questions from coming up. Since we are in most places, accidents do happen, especially on the highways of Earth. Of course, we have contact with all the Vesi through their ID chips. We are notified if there is a problem. Kind of a super OnStar system for people, or Vesi, I mean," he laughed.

"Boy, I've got a lot to learn," I said.

"You will get to see our molecular transporter next week, of course," said Milo. "It has been tested with Earth creatures, and there are hardly ever any problems. You don't mind having your atoms scattered through space, do you?"

"As long as they get put back close to where they should be," I replied, even though I wasn't so sure I was ready for this. If it worked as well as it did on *Star Trek*, I would be all right, I guessed. I didn't know how they'd do that, but right then, I could believe anything.

"Back to the DNA," Milo said. "When we arrived here, our chromosomes were a little different, and we had a few more. We learned to adjust our DNA a long time ago, making it the same number and approximately the same size as human DNA. The DNA in a body is all but impossible to change. The epigenomes, the outside chemicals, control whether the genes are active or not. We learned how to control these, and that is where genetic disorders will be controlled. Of course, having quad DNA, we can get twice as much programming done with them. If anyone made a karyotype on a Vesi, he would doubtfully notice any difference. Humans seem to think the more chromosomes, the more intelligent the creature. If that were the case, the most intelligent thing humans have discovered would be a fern that has six hundred and thirty pairs of chromosomes. There is an ant that has only one pair in the female and a single one in the males."

"I wonder if the female ants talk about how stupid the males are," I broke in.

"Most of the Earth females do," he laughed. "We will get into this a lot deeper when we have some discussions. Any quick questions?"

I paused for a moment and then asked, "Where are all the places that you have your monitoring devices?"

"The quick answer is just about everywhere. The atomic bomb surprised us. After that, we started placing them almost everywhere. You understand that we are not invading anyone's privacy since we are only studying humans and not influencing decisions that they are making. We do not get excited at human sex, as you would think we would. It is no different for the Vesi watching humans than it is for humans watching other animals. We *are* fascinated at the control it has over humans. Humans seem to exist for sex."

"Maybe it's because it's important to our existence," I said.

"It isn't that important for all the other creatures on Earth, except at reproduction time," he said. "The second greatest drive is for money, which in turn seems to be tied to more and better sex. The human pleasure center is wired completely differently from that of Vesi, not that there is anything wrong with that, but it seems to affect your entire lives. Humans are practically the only animals that have sex just for pleasure, although dolphins are known to. A few primate species, especially the bonobos, also use sex for other things than procreation."

"Do you have monitoring devices in our government facilities?" I asked.

"Of course. That's probably the most important place to have them—both in government and also military," said Milo. "After learning how some of the most important decisions in the history of the world are made, we are sometimes surprised that humans have survived this long."

"Do you have our leaders monitored?" I asked.

"Yes."

"Don't you have some form of government?" I asked.

Milo answered, "I guess you might call it that, but it's different. We have what you would call a council. Two members from each of our locations here on Earth are appointed. Sometimes, when there is an important decision that affects all the Vesi on Earth, it goes to the council for approval, and all Vesi are allowed to be involved. For example, bringing you here had to be approved by the council. Anytime humans are directly involved in our inside operations, the council has to approve it. Our abductees had to be approved by just our local representatives. I'll explain more when we have some meetings this week."

"In the video archives, do you have the history of Jesus?" I asked.

"Oh, yes," Milo said. "Many things were going on at that time, and we have most of it recorded. If it gets out, there would be many happy people and many sad people. One of these days, we will go and view that, along with the writing of the United States Constitution. If you see and hear the actual proceedings, you will find some surprises there. You will not believe some of the things we have. We could probably solve 99 percent of the crimes with the monitors and recordings we have. We aren't allowed to do that, though. Humans could do the same if they didn't have such a privacy issue. Anyway, humans are getting more and more involved with cameras and GPS tracking systems. It would be so simple to do things like put recorders in your automobiles. They could tell you every time you go over the speed limit or run a light and just send you a bill or deduct it from your account. But humans aren't going to go for it until things get really bad."

"The Vesi could cure most of our illnesses and energy problems and just about all the things we want to do someday," I said.

"Yes, but more importantly, so could humans. Do you realize that if you spent the money you do on government and military you could fix most of your problems in a decade or so? Of course, humans aren't going to go for that kind of society. One example is in geothermal energy. By drilling into the earth's crust just a few miles, you start getting heat that can be used for energy. There are a few places where it is used, but it comes to the surface there."

"A few years ago, some people were trying to drill into the core of the earth, and they got down about five miles before their drill bit started melting. How could we use this?" I asked.

"Why not just drill to the point where the heat is enough to form steam? It is already used in some places where it occurs naturally. Until you are forced by shortages or price, nothing much will ever get accomplished. The Vesi never had to go through the petroleum age, and that may be one of the reasons we developed the other forms of energy. You've only been in the petroleum age for around a century, so maybe there's hope. This place is powered by some Earth rotational generators."

"We are working on solar, wind, and battery storage," I reminded him.

"There is some work going on with batteries on the surface by humans, but the future in electrical storage is in capacitors. They charge almost instantly. The big problem is still the government and the big money people. Humans have to want to solve these problems, and until they do, these problems are just for the few who are concerned about the future, not just right now. I'm lecturing too much because I would like to see humans succeed, but I'm starting to worry. Humans were more civilized fifty years ago than they are today, and we are surprised at this revelation. We will discuss that this week. Let me show you some more things."

We walked down a corridor, and I saw many pictures on the walls. Most of them looked like weird humans. Around the universe were different species with developed intelligence and communications. There were also a few "travelers," as the Vesi call them. They are the civilizations that have interstellar travel. I saw one that looked like a human-looking reptile and one that was green.

"Little green Martian?" I asked.

"Partially correct," Milo said. "Not from Mars but from an Earth-like planet where the people are photosynthetic like the plants. About twenty percent of their energy is produced through photosynthesis like the plants use. Photosynthesis is standard throughout most of the inhabited planets. There are also many life forms like the extremophiles on Earth. They depend on chemicals for energy, like the creatures that live around the thermal vents and in the salt and sulfur ponds at Yellowstone and Rotorua, New Zealand."

"Isn't this a picture of Dr. Phil?" I asked.

"Oh, that," Milo said. "Just for fun. That is our 'Could they really be from Earth?' gallery. We have a pick of the month. In the past, we've had some people you might know of. Michael Jackson has been up there several times. Dennis Rodman, Pat Robertson, Ross Perot, Rush Limbaugh, and Glenn Beck are just a few others. You can push that spot there and thumb back through them."

I went through a bunch of them and had to agree with the Vesi. I then turned my attention back to the other pictures. "Why are so many of the intelligent species so physically similar to humans?" I asked Milo.

"Most creatures that develop intelligence have a lot in common. Walking upright is one. Most, but not all, start walking upright. It seems to have some survival benefits. One is that it frees their hands for other uses, like making and using tools and weapons. Another is that the most important senses are close to the brain in the more intelligent species. Vocal communication becomes important because more abstract ideas can be communicated.

"One of the biggest reasons the Neanderthals died out is they could not communicate as well as the Cro-Magnons due to the placement of the vocal cords. They also had twenty-four pairs of chromosomes like most other primates and couldn't interbreed easily with the Cro-Magnons and produce viable offspring. Did you know they buried their dead long before the Cro-Magnons adopted the practice? Many humans do have some Neanderthal DNA in them—mostly the humans descended from the Cro-Magnons that lived around the Neanderthals. There was limited interbreeding."

"Really?" I asked.

"Have you ever noticed that about ten percent of the population has a wild left eyebrow corner just over the nose? The eyebrow hairs there seem to have a mind of their own. That's a leftover Neanderthal gene. Start noticing it. I'm surprised that no one has made a study of it. One misspelling on one gene is what causes it. Even some people that have it don't express it because of the epigenomes that control them. The Neanderthals may have been more civilized but not as well adapted to group living as the more communicative Cro-Magnons were. We thought the humans were finished a couple of times."

"Like when?"

"When you guys left Africa, you were down to a few hundred people. You made a great recovery, but you are in the process of destroying most of the species on Earth through neglect, greed, and lack of education. There are a lot more people who don't understand that it is a group effort to maintain this planet, and when I say 'group,' I mean all the plants, animals, and people, the top animal. Here I go lecturing again. This all has to do with your mission, which I will explain to you later."

We walked on and came to a room that looked like any supply warehouse on the surface. The big difference was that the forklifts were all computer controlled, and none of them had any wheels. They operated on some sort of antigravity and didn't make a sound except when Vesi got close. Then they started beeping, just like the ones topside, to warn them. I noticed that they stopped and rose up higher when Vesi went by, but they still beeped until the Vesi were out of the possible danger of something dropping on them. They also seemed to have better and finer controls than just a forklike tine. They positioned things precisely.

"Do you all have a security system and weapons?" I asked.

Milo laughed. "No. We have security in the fact we know what is going on everywhere on Earth. We have all the world leaders monitored—both good and bad. As for weapons, we never developed them, except for hunting, which we did long before we learned how to raise our food. We never had wars and very little crime after we learned to provide for everyone. Everyone cooperated in the production of our society also. The last criminal we had was about a hundred thousand years ago. Someone took an item from another Vesi without permission."

"What happened to him?" I asked.

"That DNA was never used again for anything. Out of the pool, so to speak," Milo said. "The Vesi was exiled to a planet that has not yet developed intelligent life but which would sustain him for the rest of his life alone. No way to leave, communicate, or escape. I can't imagine anything worse happening to a Vesi. But we have rules, and everyone understands from almost birth what the limits are. We figured it had to be a DNA flaw since no other Vesi seemed to have the problem."

"You mean you're defenseless?" I asked.

"We would leave if we had to before we would give our technology to an uncertified civilization like humans are at the present," Milo said. "We would have to destroy it all before surrendering it. That is why we do not normally allow it on the surface. Our ID chips and monitoring devices are there, but they will not be discovered or figured out for centuries. Some of it would destroy itself if you tried to use it improperly. The antigravity power plants are dangerous if used incorrectly, and the picotechnology is far too advanced for humans to figure out with your present technology. You all haven't figured out the atom correctly yet. Maybe someday soon you will do that and then develop technology to see what's going on. As soon as someone discovers something great, he will sell the rights to it and retire to his mansions, sports cars, and boats, never to be heard from again. Social control is money and sex. I guess that our not developing as great of a sex drive as humans has also led to our success. We are also a lot older, so maybe I'm being too critical of you young'uns." He laughed.

"Let me show you our satellite system," Milo said.

"You have satellites? Why haven't we detected them?" I asked.

"Our satellites are around eighty thousand miles out, and they are not radar reflective. They were passed on the moon missions, but being flat black, they are extremely difficult to see. We have thousands of them that are used for communication, sensing, and other scientific purposes. They are about the size of basketballs, or smaller, and use subatomic communications. You are centuries away from that form of communication.

"Most communicating civilizations have advanced past the radio frequency communications, and that is one reason you are having such a hard time picking up other civilizations. You have people spending their lives listening for transmissions from some other life form. The only problem is that you are listening in the frequency ranges used by humans. If the aliens were transmitting on these frequencies and with these types of technologies, then they would be no more advanced than Earth is. What you are looking for is another Earth. The residents would not be able to travel to each other or communicate, for that matter, since you are presently stuck with the speed of light. The signals are also so weak over the vast distances, and the chance of locating one over these distances is remote. The fact that you are looking is good, but you must start to consider what an alien would do.

"Most scientists are not open to the faster-than-light theory. At one time, the earth was flat and only a few thousand years old. Most scientists have gotten past this. They still have a few hurdles, and they will be working on dark energy and dark matter. Dark energy and matter is just the opposite of what it really is. It isn't dark, just not visible. Then again, germs were invisible a short time ago. More lecture."

"I don't take is as lecture but as learning. I love the translator that was implanted, but why don't you have one that translates what I say into another language?" I asked.

"Believe me, we tried. We worked on them for centuries but were never successful. There is too much involved in speech—the brain, vocal cords, lips, tongue, and all the other attaching parts. Each person is unique, and we had a few developed, but everyone always sounded like Bob Dylan, so we never understood what was being said. By the way, that's something you'll have to remember. I would suggest you keep yours off unless you want to eavesdrop on someone—and you might be thinking others are speaking English when they're not. Living in Florida, there is a good chance they're not.

"We have a great deal of other technology that you may occasionally run into, and we will go over it when we need to," Milo continued. "I want you to think of questions you want to ask about us or about human history for the next time we meet. You have to consider whether you want to continue visiting with us or not. You are not captive, and can stop anytime you wish. But if we have you figured correctly, you will not be able to keep from finding out what has happened in the past. I wish we knew what was going to happen in the future, but we have never found any way to go there. We cannot go backward either, except with recordings of what has happened. There is a lot of information, and our DNA records are impressive, if I must say so myself."

"What's my mission going to be?" I asked.

"I can't ask you to do it just yet," Milo said. "You need to analyze what has happened so far and decide if you want to be involved or not. If everything goes well, I should be able to ask you if you are interested in the mission after next weekend. We probably should get you back topside so you can prep for school tomorrow and see the animals. So if there are no questions that have to be answered right now, we should proceed back."

"Just one observation I would like to know about. I noticed that in the cafeterias, the Vesi seem to cook and do things just like we do. Is there a reason? Couldn't the technology be advanced for that?"

"Sure it can, and it was," Milo said. "We had microwave-type ovens that cooked all kinds of things instantly. We realized after a while that the one thing we had to spare was a lot of time, so the microwaves mostly have been abandoned, except in our long-range craft, where we sometimes are on a schedule and don't want to waste time with food prep. We dropped laser knives centuries ago since there were so many accidents with them. We could never keep the laser range to just a knife length, so we just kept it simple. Many times we dropped technology and used the KISS method—Keep it simple, stupid. Works well for most situations.

"There's another technology that you have been in contact with but may not have realized its importance," he continued. "What do you think our transporters are made from?"

"I figured they were some sort of super metal or alloy," I said.

Milo replied, "They have some metal in them, but they are almost entirely carbon. Most of the things we use are composed of carbon nano and pico structures. There is some metal interwoven into it. That's one of the reasons they are radar invisible. It's also the reason we can make the outside appear to have windows, lights, or anything for that matter. That is how some travelers' crafts, or UFOs, seem to disappear. They just make the surface look like the background. If fact, most of the things you see are mostly carbon or silicon with other elements added. The carbon cooperates so great with manufacturing since it pretty much assembles itself once it is started. Silicon is also great but harder to work with than carbon.

"Would you like to see something weird?" Milo asked.

I stopped dead in my tracks, looked straight at Milo, and said, "I've seen a spaceship, abduction, and crop circles. I've seen aliens dressed as other aliens, I met a talking grocery-shopping dolphin, and now you want to show me something weird, is this correct?"

"Well, I sort of think it's strange," he said. "Not everything we do has a significant scientific purpose; sometimes it's just for entertainment and fun."

"What do I have to lose?" I asked.

We walked down a hallway and entered a large room with floor-to-ceiling screens, like an IMAX theater but larger and completely surrounded with screens, or perhaps I should say *a* screen. Vesi were watching a NASCAR race, and almost everyone was wearing a pit crew uniform from a different team. They were really getting into it. I noticed that in several areas, someone was in what looked like a NASCAR race car, and everyone was wearing racing suits, helmets, gloves … everything. The cars were bouncing as if they were actually in a race. It sounded just like the track. I had been to Daytona several times, and I occasionally watched the races on television.

"Lots of our people—I call them people in English for simplicity—love racing, NASCAR especially," Milo explained. "The videos were done at the actual races, and if you are here on Sunday, they will have a live holographic video of the race. The ones in the cars are getting a video from this race from actual drivers' helmets, and it is exactly what the drivers' eyes are seeing. We have cameras and an iris-tracking device on some drivers, and no, they have no idea. Wait until I show you some of our technology, and you will understand better.

"You can even get into the driver's seat with them—only on video, though," he continued. "It is real time and these guys have their favorites, of course. Dale Jr. seems to be the favorite, but the others also have good followings. If you heard these guys on race days you would think they were regular humans. They argue whose driver is the best, and which cars and tracks are the best. We can do this for most sporting events where the athletes wear helmets or caps. Football is also a favorite, along with horse racing and a few others. One of the fun things is to be an umpire or referee in a game and see exactly what they see. These sporting events are the only times you will hear us disagreeing with each other. The rest of the time, everyone is on the same track with the same objectives."

I was thinking of just how rich I could be with something like that. Oh well. If I'd wanted to be rich, I never would have gone into teaching, which I had to keep telling myself. This whole thing could be a new attraction from Disney or Sea World, but the thing with Sam doing what I asked him made me think it's real.

We walked to the place where we'd started the adventure, going into the small hangar where the first small craft was parked. After we boarded the craft, the hangar filled with water, and the outer door opened. Milo gave the craft instructions to take us to the school, where they had taken my car. There was no one around the school, but I had forgotten that they locked the gates at night. I didn't know what we were going to do, but as soon as we got there, Milo saw the problem.

He took manual control of the craft. He pressed a few buttons, and one of the small things that had made the crop circles and fixed the tracks at the abduction departed and went under my car, lifted it, and set it down outside the gates. That was cool! The craft then hovered close to the ground, the door opened, and I departed. Milo said he would be in touch, telling me to make a list of questions I would like to have answered. I started thinking about that on my way home but decided to wait until I had time to absorb all that had happened.

I arrived home to a resounding chorus of tail wagging and two cats looking at me as if to say, *And where have you been so long? We could have starved, you know.* I took a shower, reacquainted myself with Ralph and Hide and Seek, and watched a little of the late news. Since I noticed I wasn't on it, I thought I'd get some sleep since it was going to be a strange week. I dropped off to sleep with all the livestock in bed with me.

Chapter Nine: Topside Meeting

I woke up Monday morning and went through my normal routine. I got everyone fed, taken out, and the cat box cleaned, and then I went off to school. I have to admit that I thought I would have a difficult time concentrating or avoiding getting excited and saying, "Guess what I did this weekend!" After a few minutes into the first class, I realized the kids would either not believe or not care. It was about fifty-fifty probably.

Anyway, I got through the day and avoided saying anything unusual to any of the other teachers. I thought about it and then figured they would be about the same as the students. They were all wrapped up in their classes or personal lives, so generally they weren't that interested in anything new. A couple of the teachers tried to keep up on the latest news from the science world, but most of them would be content to teach the same tried-and-true lesson plans they had used since they started teaching. Most all of the lesson plans fit into the time schedule, and most all the questions had already been addressed years earlier. No sense in rocking the boat or reinventing the wheel, as they would say. If they only knew what was really going on in the world, they might not sleep so easily in the teachers' lounge.

I got home and took care of the animals, which had been there all day, and got all the welcomes out of the way. I started to think about what I might scare up for my dinner. I wished I could drop into one of the cafeterias downside because they sure had good food. I found out from Milo that most of the cooks had spent some time in culinary schools and in some of the greatest restaurants around the world.

I had just decided to get a sub sandwich when the phone rang. It was Milo. He said he would be visiting tomorrow and asked if I would mind grilling a couple of steaks for us. I said that would be no problem. We chatted a bit about how the day had gone and if I had been able to sleep. In case people asked about him, he told me just to say that he was a teacher I had met on a school trip, and to tell them his name was Milo—but I had forgotten the last name, if I had ever known it. He reminded me to make a list of questions I might have, saying that he would try to answer them.

After going to get a sub, I brought it home since Ralph thought he should have part of anything I ate. Some veterinarians say you shouldn't do that, but Ralph seemed to enjoy it so much that I would never want to disappoint him. Ralph and I ate our sub, and I listened to the news while we were doing it. It sure was lonely most of the time since Karol had died, but the animals were good company. Of course, there was nothing much on the news except bad stuff, but then again, that's their job. Nobody wants to hear about the thirty to forty thousand planes that make a safe landing every day, but everyone will stop and look at the one that did not. Human nature, I guess.

After dinner, I took Ralph for a walk and started thinking about questions I wanted to ask Milo. I thought I might go chronologically, and then I thought I might go in order of importance to me, and then I thought I didn't know how I would go. I just started mentally jotting them down in the order I thought of them.

Does God exist? Was Jesus real? What caused the other mass extinctions before the dinosaurs? Are there other alien races visiting Earth? Where is Jimmy Hoffa? Where is Osama? Who put the bomp in the bomp, bomp, bomp? Maybe that one I would throw out. What is my so-called mission? Are we really going to the moon and Mars, and does their transporter hurt in any way? Why do they say humans aren't civilized yet? Of course, if you watch the news you could probably answer that yourself. I figured I'd probably think of a few more once I started talking to Milo.

The next day at school was more normal, and I occasionally thought of a few other questions I wanted answered. I couldn't wait for the day to end, though, and on the way home, I stopped at the store and picked up a couple of steaks and some ready-made baked potatoes. I already had plenty of beer, wine, tea, coffee, or whatever Milo might want. Of course, it wasn't going to be like the food down below, but I didn't think he was coming for the food. I got a few things ready and watched the early news. Ralph was unusually happy because he could smell the steaks, I guess. I thought he was going to wear his tail out wagging it. He knew he would get to spend the evening with a nice meaty bone.

I heard a car pull up in front and then a knock on the door. It was Milo, and he handed me a bottle of wine. I was a 1996 Barolo red that I knew would be good. I invited him in, and Ralph ran to greet him, acting like he was an old friend, but Hide and Seek decided they would find a bed to hide under until this whole mess was over. Milo came in, looked around, and told me I had a nice place, as expected, and I invited him on through the house to the patio area. I had a fairly large patio and pool area that backed to a golf course. I rarely played, but it was good not having neighbors right behind me.

It was a wonderful evening. The afternoon rain had cooled the air a lot, and it didn't seem so humid, but I'm sure it was by some standards. We talked a little about the neighbors and the golf course, and Milo said he had played a few times, but it was hard to get into hitting a ball, going and finding it, and hitting it again. I told Milo the object of the game was to see how many times you could do that without throwing a club or swearing, and he laughed and said now he understood.

I put the steaks on the grill and offered Milo a drink; he said a scotch and water would be fine. I fixed us both one, and we opened the wine to let it breathe before dinner. I couldn't wait to enjoy it. I'd had a Barolo once before, and it was an excellent wine. I asked Milo where he had gotten it, and he said it had come from Italy yesterday. He had ordered it through their supply channels, and I was wishing I had access to that. Maybe someday.

When dinner was ready, Milo poured the Barolo, and I was not disappointed. It was excellent. I wondered if Italian winos ever got hold of any of the good stuff. I then wondered if they had Ripple and Thunderbird in Italy. I sometimes thought that my mind must have a leak in it.

Meanwhile, Ralph was sitting on the floor and staring a hole in me. He watched every bite, and just in case one fell out, it would never make it to the floor. I gave him a few small pieces, and he ate them with much gusto and got back into position.

"Next time I come, I'll bring some Kobe beef for us," Milo said. "I could have it in a few hours, but I usually like to give a day's notice for special orders. We have plenty downside, but I like to get it fresh whenever I need it."

We finished up, and I offered Milo an after-dinner brandy. He accepted. I gave Ralph his bone, and he took it to a safe place about ten feet from us, settling down for an evening of bone cleaning. Milo pulled out a couple of Cuban Cohibas and gave me one.

"These aren't as good as they were thirty to forty years ago, and many of the Central American–made ones were just as good," he said. But the idea that they were Cuban made them good. We were just settling down with our brandy and cigars when the doorbell rang.

It was Troy, and I invited him in. I introduced him to Milo and told him he was a teacher I had met at a seminar. I left it at that. I didn't know if this irritated Milo or not.

Milo asked, "Troy, would you like a cigar?" I offered him a brandy also.

"I would love that if it's not an intrusion," Troy answered. He was here to tell me that there was a plant sale this weekend, and he knew I was looking for some new landscaping plants. Troy was in real estate, and we chatted a bit about how the landscaping helped the value of a house. He and Linda had moved in shortly after Karol and I had, and they had been good friends. I hadn't seen much of her after Karol died, and I think she felt uneasy since she and Karol had been close. Troy was always looking after me because he thought that without Karol, I wouldn't know what to do most of the time. He was partially right. We engaged in small talk until the cigars were about dead and Troy went home. Then it was time for Milo and me to have a real chat. I got my list of questions.

"You're not driving, are you?" I asked before I poured another brandy for each of us.

"Not a chance," he replied with a slight laugh.

"Good," I said, and we sat back and got ready for a discussion. "The first question I have is whether God exists or not."

Milo took a small sip of brandy and looked away as if deep in thought for a moment. Looking at me again, he said, "That is a definite maybe. I mean, we have never found any proof that there is a single god-type person or entity. The Vesi believe there is a power that made the universes—yes, plural—but we don't see him or her, or it, as somebody you ask for a raise or to help you get a good grade or promotion. We believe that he—and I'm referring to God as *he* just for simplicity—is the power that created the universe and all the forces in it. We can't even imagine what there was before the universes were created, and we still have limited knowledge of what is in any other universes."

He continued, "We see everything as a form of energy. All the particles of the atoms, and we are discovering smaller and smaller particles, are made of energy. We have no idea how small or how large things might be. We are a lot more logical than humans in our thinking.

"Humans have used God as social control for what seems like forever. Humans can't accept the idea that they are responsible for their own actions, and each seems to think his god is the only right one. There are probably a few dozen gods on the earth right now, but that is down from a few hundred in earlier times. Not all these gods can be the true one. There is no agreement even within each religious group about the workings of their god. There are all degrees of beliefs and practices in every religious group.

"We Vesi believe that we should treat everyone the same, and the basic law is to treat others the way you like to be treated. If we just stick to that one premise, then the others are not needed. For example, all ten of the Christian commandments would be covered by it. But you have to actually do it and not just say you believe. Most of the earth's religions, and elsewhere in the universe, I might add, are based on faith alone. That would be fine except they all differ. Everyone has the one true god, and he tells the people to get rid of all the others. We believe more in doing than just blind faith. We could discuss the various religions for hours, weeks, years, or centuries and come to no conclusion as to who is right. We don't even know if we're right, but it seems to work for us, and everyone seems to be equal. We don't continually have wars to prove we are right. Is that anywhere close to what you needed to know about God, or a lack thereof?" he asked.

"Yes, more or less," I said. "Along the same line, my next question is whether there was a real Jesus."

"That one's easier to answer," Milo said. "Yes, there was. Was he born of a virgin? Was he the son of God? Some of these questions we cannot answer. We weren't monitoring Mary and Joseph, and the only clues we have are the recordings, which will take you weeks to watch and maybe bring you more questions than answers. You need to plan a long weekend or maybe even a week to see them, and many of your questions will be answered. I can tell you for sure that you are in for some surprises. Just let me know when you can go downside for a longer stay. Fair enough?"

"Fair enough," I said, but I wondered if I truly wanted to know some of these things. "Next question on my list is what caused another mass extinction about two hundred and fifty million years ago, before the one that killed the dinosaurs? Was it another meteorite?"

"No, that one wasn't a meteorite like the dinosaur killer," Milo said. "It was caused by massive volcanoes in what is now Siberia, which in turn raised the earth's temperature several degrees, releasing trapped carbon dioxide from the ocean floors and slowly killing most of the vegetation and animal life on Earth. This took sixty to eighty million years, whereas the dino killing was overnight, geologically speaking. We have video, you know."

"Next, what were the Founding Fathers of America thinking when they wrote the Declaration and Constitution?" I asked.

"That is one recording I wish all Americans could see, but it isn't possible—at this point in time anyway," Milo said. "There are many surprises there, but you have to remember that was over a couple of hundred years ago. There have been many changes in human technology since the Founding Fathers were discussing these. You would be surprised at some of the discussions. You will find that they did not envision machine guns and those types of weapons when they were insuring the right to bear arms. Some of these were simple, religious people, and most were ancestors of people whom did not agree with how things were run in their home countries. Some others left because they did not agree with the forced religions at the time. Again, you need to spend some time in the video library and get a few surprises."

"I see I may have to spend some free time downside," I said.

"Actually, you need to spend a lot of time there," Milo answered.

Ralph came over and looked at me, and I knew he needed to go out. I needed to take a break also.

"Let me take Ralph out for a few minutes and see what he has to say about this so far," I said jokingly.

"Of course. It's always good to get a second opinion," Milo said with a chuckle.

I took Ralph out to do his business and asked him about some things. He just looked at me as if I were crazy. He could possibly be right.

Ralph and I came back in, and I sat back down and went on to my next question. "Where did the first humans arise, and how did they populate the earth?" I asked.

"Most of that is in the process of being answered by humans now. The short answer is that intelligent humans originated in what is now Africa and migrated out of there to almost every place on Earth. A few remaining tribes around the earth aren't that far advanced from when their ancestors left there. They will probably disappear within the next fifty years, though. Human progress is killing them, along with most other animal species around the world.

"Your DNA discoveries are leading to finding how the earth was populated, and I think it is great that you humans are finally finding out your backgrounds. At one time, humans were down to around several hundred people worldwide, and we thought you were goners. You surprised us by not only surviving but prospering as well. That's one of the reasons we took a special interest in humans. Most other intelligent races around the universe didn't have such a hard time existing. It will be a shame to see that the more intelligent the species gets, the more apt it is to destroy itself."

"What's the story of Roswell?" I asked.

"Funny you should ask. Roswell was real. Of course it was real; it's still there," he laughed. "What I mean is that it was a real spacecraft crash. Not one of ours but a scout ship from another race, which was checking Earth out for settlement. We removed most of the craft and bodies from Area 51 because humans were not ready for the truth yet. Later, we realized that we were interfering with developments on Earth, and after a long council meeting, we decided what we did was wrong, by our standards, and that we will not interfere if it happens again … and it will. Remember, this was just after World War II and the first use of atomic weapons against humans. We were still a bit unsettled, and everyone on Earth was trying to get 'the bomb.' They were from a planet in the Milky Way, not far from Earth, astronomically speaking," he added.

"Next question. Are there any other alien races visiting Earth right now?" I asked.

"If you mean like the Vesi, the answer is most likely not. They could be further advanced than we are, so they could be here and we might not know, it but I doubt it. We haven't had any reason to think they are.

"As far as past visitors, the answer is yes. There have been several different races visiting here, but they didn't stay long. Some of them couldn't adapt to the gravity, and some of them couldn't adapt to the atmosphere. From what we know of them, they didn't manipulate their genetics to fit the place the way we have. It would be like humans trying to adapt to the Martian atmosphere and gravity; it would be quite difficult. A few of them tried to set up colonies here with some of the ancient cultures, especially in Central and South America. It just didn't work because the humans thought they were gods. Some visitors designed the Pyramids and aided somewhat in the transportation of the stones, but mostly they showed the people how to move them using the items they had available. It still took thousands of people and centuries to build. If you check the alignment of the Pyramids with stars, you can find where they were from. Their problem was climate. The earth was too cold for them, so finally they gave up and moved on. They really needed a planet warmer and a bit larger than Earth.

"Did we ever contact them? No, we just monitored them and were glad they left because they were starting to influence humans. They actually caused some of the ancient cultures to die out by providing food, and the people stopped learning how to fend for themselves. When the aliens departed, the races were somewhat helpless. You can watch some of these videos, and it gets depressing sometimes. They felt these aliens were gods and started killing people as sacrifices, thinking it would bring them back. That is the reason they built altars as high as they could, to get closer to where the gods went."

"I'll check out some of those videos," I said. "Can you tell me where Jimmy Hoffa went? What about Osama?"

Milo laughed. "Jimmy Hoffa is in Kalamazoo with Elvis, working at Burger King. Not really. He is up in smoke. He was killed and cremated in Detroit. He never went to a farm. His ashes did so they couldn't be used in any way for testing.

"As far as Osama is concerned, I'll check and see." Milo then said something in Vesi that I couldn't understand since I had my translators off. The translators are constantly monitored, and you only had to speak to have someone send you an answer. We waited, and after a few seconds, Milo said, "Right now he's in Iran. Close to the border with Afghanistan and Pakistan. That whole area is a toss-up as to where the borders are, and they are governed by local warlords who are still living in the fifteenth century, except with modern weapons. He moves a lot because he is afraid the satellites will find him and bomb him. He is right, of course. I could give you his GPS coordinates, but by the time you found someone who would listen, he would be a hundred miles from there. He will probably die on his own before he is killed. He is not a well man, but he is surprisingly resilient."

I looked out the window, and that brought up another question. "Can you control the weather?" I asked.

"To a limited degree," Milo said. "We can do things like make it rain if there is sufficient moisture in the air. We can't steer hurricanes or tornadoes or precisely predict earthquakes, but we are close to predicting them and volcanoes. The earth is heating up due to global warming, and the more it heats up, the more active it gets. A few degrees will cause it to expand; increasing the earthquakes and volcanoes, and the warmer oceans will cause more hurricanes and coral die-offs. It's a vicious cycle, but it can be a learning experience."

"Is there anything mysterious about the Bermuda Triangle?" I asked.

"Nothing supernatural. Just a lot of traffic and some piracy of boats, but no real creatures grabbing people out of the sky or off the water. There are a lot of thunderstorms that come up quickly and sink small boats."

"Next up, Bigfoot and Loch Ness?" I asked.

"Loch Ness is a total nonstarter. Nothing there, never was, isn't now," Milo answered. "Now, Bigfoot is real, but none of the videos that have been shown are real. We do have some you can see. There were never many of these yetis, and there are only a few left now—mostly in the northwestern United States and lower Canada, and a few are left in the Himalayas. The problem is that there are twelve males and three females in North America, and they are probably scattered too far apart ever to find each other. They are remnants of the Gigantopithecus species, but they were never very successful as a group. They do tend to live for up to one hundred fifty years but never developed much intelligence and are terribly shy, even with each other."

"Now for a big question," I said. "How do the Vesi reproduce? You have hinted that it isn't exactly like humans."

"Okay. Sit down, relax, and let me see if I can simplify this," Milo said. "We Vesi started like humans with sexual reproduction. Our sex drive wasn't as great as that of humans since we didn't have such a competitive spirit for mates. We learned early on to only have enough offspring to basically replace ourselves and grow somewhat as conditions and technologies improved to support the additional numbers. I believe that only having the one continent helped in that we didn't develop different nations and different religions that resulted in expansive wars and governments. Also, we never had a petroleum energy–based life. We used geothermal, nuclear, solar, wind, and even the earth's rotation and gravity for power sources. Early on, we developed a sharing sort of economy, and there was no reason for accumulating huge wealth. Everyone was pretty much the same. It is tremendously expensive to have wars and governments. Most wars are the results of religions, economics, or egos—sometimes a combination of these.

"To get back to reproduction, once we learned about gene manipulation, we started doing mostly in-vitro fertilization. We also learned that it is safer and easier to nourish the fetus in an artificial womb egg outside the female. All we needed was the DNA from each parent, and we could have the whole process taken care of outside the womb. We were more like the other animals, only having sex for procreation and not so much for recreation. Humans are obsessed with sex, and it requires so much of your energy, but in a way, it's not your fault. The human pleasure center is so much more controlling than ours is. The drug problems are directly related to your pleasure center. The accumulation of wealth and possessions is directly related to your pleasure center. Your quest for control and power is directly related to your pleasure center, and even helping other people gives some humans great pleasure."

Milo continued, "We select our offsprings' characteristics and have them approved in advance when it is time, which is almost always later in our lifetimes. Then our DNA is used in an artificial womb that is controlled, and there are seldom any problems. There have been some, but they were so minor that they were statistically unimportant. A by-product of this was that after a few hundred generations, the females actually stopped developing fertile eggs and stopped having real cycles. They still have the hormone cycles but not the mess, and they can control the hormones if they want to. In case we find problems with our methods down the road, we have civilizations on a few planets where Vesi reproduce in the old biological method. On these planets, we are the only intelligent species.

"Sex for us is different since there isn't really marriage, as there is in human societies. We do have a thing like love, but it is based more on logic and enjoyment of being with someone, rather than for sex and possession, as human marriages seem to be. So that's the Cliff Notes version. You can see some of the processes sometime when you're downside," he added.

"Fair enough. I see I may be visiting a few times. My next question is where are all the Vesi on the surface?" I asked.

"Well, that's a hard one," Milo said. "We're pretty much everywhere. A lot of the Vesi are helping in our supply system, and some are just observers. Actually, all Vesi are observers, but some are assigned that as a primary mission. We have Vesi in most walks of human life, with the exception of positions of power, like military and government. Also, we do not get into education because it can influence humans.

"We have a few rules, and one is that there are no children involved, either Vesi or human. The couples will always be childless, and they do not adopt either. Many Vesi are single. We have no problem creating histories and identifications for our people. Your computers are still quite rudimentary. Our computers learn as we do and consult with each other; they are almost lifelike."

"Why don't you guys just take over?" I asked.

"Why? That isn't what we're here for. In the Milky Way alone, we could live on a few thousand planets just like Earth. We're observing and learning. We have an insatiable quest for knowledge and have never been interested in controlling anywhere. We want to know about the other universes and to establish travel there and back someday."

"Are we really going to the moon and Mars this weekend?" I asked.

"If you're still interested, we are," Milo said.

"Are you kidding me? I wouldn't miss it for anything, but I'm worried about the transporter. What if I get scattered all over space?"

Milo laughed. "Don't worry. We get most of the parts back in the right place most of the time."

I knew he was kidding again, or I hoped so anyway. "And now I would like to know why the Vesi think humans aren't civilized yet," I said. I stood up and paced around a little, and I was sure that Milo could tell I was irritated at this perceived dig on humans. "We have cured many diseases, helped people with deformities, and stopped tyrants like Hitler. Humans have done, and are in the process of doing, lots of good things."

"Maybe we should have a glass of water and also a couple more cigars since this might take awhile," Milo said. Milo followed me into the kitchen, and I got him a glass of water and a Coke for myself. We returned to our seats.

"Just sit back and relax," Milo said. "We have much respect for humans or I would not be here." Milo stared straight ahead for a few moments, as if getting his thoughts straight. "Yes, you have, and I might add that there are a lot of civilized humans, but speaking as a group, the humans are actually degrading themselves as a species. In the nineteen fifties and sixties, humans were actually more civilized as a species than they are now. World War II was over, and most of the earth was settled down. Great strides were being made in rebuilding all the ruin of the war, and economies were taking off."

"That was supposed to be our greatest generation," I added.

"There were great advances in electronics, medicine, almost everything. The fifties were the start of new music, and there was great hope for the world. The start of space exploration was getting underway, and we thought that you might actually make it. Then it seemed like there was an overnight increase in greed and religions, and the next thing we knew, there were wars and genocide everywhere—and hatred between what seemed like every group. More humans die in the names of their gods than anything. There have always been religious wars on Earth, but it seems to have gotten far too dangerous with the new technologies."

"Somewhat true," I said.

"The new technologies also brought great harm to the earth's environment. That is dangerous for humans since you all have nowhere else to go. If things get really bad, we Vesi could just leave. We do not want to since we have developed a real fondness for humans. They are one of the most interesting groups in the universe. They are so contradictory, and they constantly surprise the logical Vesi mind. We are fascinated at how this is going to turn out. Remember, we are in for the long haul. Humans were down to a few hundred and rallied back, so we think there is a possibility that you may actually survive.

"We can't figure out a few things, though," Milo continued. "Humans continually weaken the species by sanitizing everything too much so the immune system never gets the practice it used to. Children play inside and are never in contact with germs like in the earlier days, so the immune systems are weakened. As soon as there is any kind of indication of illness, antibiotics are used, so nature is left out. Humans straighten teeth, fix vision, correct hearing, and take care of other problems that would have eliminated many people from reproducing in the old days. The DNA base is also being weakened because the more responsible and intelligent humans are reproducing fewer offspring than most of those who are less educated and less responsible. Pesticides and plastics are in almost everything you eat, and pharmaceuticals are showing up all over nature. So many health problems can be traced to some of these.

"There are genocides all over the world, and religious fanatics on all sides are causing problems everywhere," he continued. "You are ruining your environment with chemicals and pollution, and the people who control those also control the government through campaign money and power. We hope that before it is too late, humans will realize what they are doing and get involved in fixing the problems. Sounds like I'm preaching or running for office, but this is real and needs fixed pretty fast. Does any of this sound familiar?"

"Yes, lots of it, but humans don't seem to respond until they are in a corner. They don't want to think of the future. As a group, we are a *today* species."

We sat and relaxed and I thought about some of our discussions. As always in science, the more you learn, the more questions you have. Milo looked at me as if he could tell I was deep in thought and probably needed to digest some of the things we discussed. He was right, of course.

"I'll be going now," Milo said, handing me a card. "I'll give you some time to think about some of these things. If you need to get in touch with me, just call the number on the card—or you could turn your translators on and ask for me."

"What's this mission you mentioned? I asked.

"I want to wait until you come downside again before we ask you to do it," Milo replied.

"Is it anything I should be concerned about?" I inquired.

"Not for now. It will require you to do some thinking, but it is quite simple. You don't have enough background for it yet, but you will. Don't worry about it now."

We said our good-byes, and Milo went outside to a waiting taxi that I never heard him call, nor heard drive up, but then again, nothing much surprised me anymore. As Milo departed, I wondered if the taxi driver was Vesi.

I took Ralph out one last time before bed, and we were both ready to get a few winks. Hide and Seek came out, sniffed around, and did not like the cigar smell at all. They would survive. They still came into the bedroom with Ralph and me, and we all drifted off.

Chapter Ten: To the Moon, Alice!

It had been a few days since I had any contact with Milo, but I figured he would contact me eventually, so I didn't worry. I went to school and tried to keep focused on the lesson and the plans for the semester, but it wasn't easy. Every so often, we would come across something in the book, and I'd almost say, "This isn't completely true." But I had decided to try not to challenge anything in the books, at least not yet. The students had some interesting questions, and sometimes it was hard not to try to explain some of the things I had seen. Of course, I also had a few students who didn't believe anything I said about the age of the earth or the solar system, and that was fine too. I just reminded them that for the purpose of school and tests, the information they got from the book and class would be considered correct.

Finally, on Thursday night, I heard from Milo, and he asked if I still wanted to go. I said I did, and he reminded me to get someone to look after the livestock for the weekend. I thought I would ask Troy again since he was so dependable. *I must remember to get him a gift,* I thought. *A moon rock, maybe?* I guess that might be hard to prove or explain. He seemed to really enjoy those cigars Milo had brought, so maybe I could ask Milo if it would be possible to get a few of those for him. I called Troy, and he said it was no problem.

Troy said, "You sure are spending a lot of time at conferences lately. Maybe you've found another teacher to spend some quality time with, if you know what I mean."

"I can assure you that is not the case. These conferences are educational from a scientific point of view, if you know what *I* mean," I replied.

I would have loved to tell him what was going on, but I knew that was out of the question. Anyway, he would try to put a For Sale sign on the moon if he could. Realtors never changed.

Milo had said for me to just go to the airport and leave my car there after school, and he would pick me up there. I asked him where to meet, and he said not to worry. He would be at my car within a couple of minutes after I parked. I had forgotten that they were able to track me with my implants. I thought these should be in everyone. We would know exactly who was at the scene of the crime at all times. Crime could be eliminated in short order, but the freedom screamers would be outraged. Maybe when we become civilized, it might happen. The more I thought about things like that, the more I realized that Milo was probably right about our not being civilized.

On Friday, school was almost a waste for me. I was so anxious, and I knew the students could tell. They asked me if I had a date for the weekend, and I said I sort of did, but it was education based and not romantic, and they all groaned like I was nuts. *If they only knew.* I showed a film to the class, and then they did independent study, which is school board talk for relax and be quite until the dismissal bell. During the film, I required them to take notes and hand them in for a homework grade, and if nothing else, it kept most of them awake.

After school, I started to go home for some clothes, and then I remembered that I wouldn't need them. I went anyway and said good-bye to the animals and Troy. I then drove to the airport and into the long-term parking lot. I found an empty space and put my ticket over the visor so I would know where it was when I returned. I had just about secured everything when Milo drove up. I asked where we were going, and he said we would stop and have a light meal and wait until it started to get darker.

We stopped at a small pizza stand along the beach and each had a slice of pizza. We then walked down to the beach, and it started getting dark. Soon we were alone on the beach, and the craft was coming across the water toward us. We got in and were gone in just a few seconds, submerging fairly quickly. We went down into the small hangar we had originally gone into on my first trip. We went inside and walked through the halls until we came to a small room that had what looked like a rounded elevator on one side. There were a couple of racks of coveralls and several small changing rooms. Milo gave me what looked like a Depends and I stared at it.

"Put this on instead of your underwear," he said.

"Is it going to be that scary?" I asked.

He laughed hard for a few seconds and then said, "These are like Depends, but they have special filler that can absorb a day's worth of urine, and they stay dry. You know, there are very few rest areas in space." He laughed again.

I went in and put it on. It felt weird, but I stopped noticing it almost immediately, as it seemed to adapt itself to me. I put on the coveralls I had taken off the rack. They were complete with booties. My size exactly, of course. I came out, and Milo handed me a pair of what looked like swimming goggles, telling me to put them on. I was starting to get extremely nervous. Milo noticed and said, "Just relax." The lenses of the goggles were almost black from the outside, but when I put them on, I could see as if they weren't there.

Milo then said in his best Captain Kirk voice, "Well, Mac, are you ready to have your atoms scattered all over space?" Then he laughed. I didn't think it was that funny. He motioned me into the room that looked like a large elevator, and I noticed that there were a few white spots on the floor. They were round and about two feet in diameter. He motioned for me to stand on one, and he stood on another one.

"Hold still for a moment," he cautioned, and then he said, "Ready?" The lights went down low, and I noticed what looked like several fluorescent lights, which were slightly different colors, going completely around us, from the ceiling to the floor and back, in what was probably a minute total. I felt a little tingling over my skin and noticed my heart was beating hard enough to break a rib. When the lights returned to the ceiling, they went off, and the interior lights came back on gradually. The door on the opposite side of the room opened, and Milo motioned me out. He took off his goggles and said, "That wasn't too bad, was it?"

"No, but where are we? Are we on the moon?" I asked.

"No, not yet, but you're germ free," he laughed. "We don't have a transporter like *Star Trek* had. We tried to invent one, and were successful at disassembling things, including organisms, but could never get them together again. Humpty Dumpty doesn't want to fall down here. We have never met another civilization that ever got one to work either, but we still have people trying as more of a hobby. We never leave the planet without sterilizing people and equipment, so we don't contaminate another world, or return without sterilizing everything before reentering. As soon as we get to the edge of space, you can see the procedure. Personally, I think it's cool."

We walked out of that room and into a large hangar that had a still larger version of their craft. It seemed they were all pretty much the same, except for the size and interiors. We boarded the craft and walked into the control center; there were three other Vesi in there. One was probably the tallest black female I had ever seen. One of the others looked Asian, and the other appeared to be Caucasian. I'm sure I looked surprised, for Milo laughed again. It seemed he was enjoying my education.

Milo introduced me to them. My translators had been turned on when I had arrived at the airport parking lot, so it was as though everyone was speaking English.

The tall female held her hand out and said, "Hello, I'm Captain Winslow but please call me Stretch. That's what everybody calls me. I'll be your voyager, or pilot, if you prefer, this weekend."

The Asian-looking "person" held out his hand and said, "Welcome aboard. I'm the copilot-slash-navigator-slash-computer operator. My name is Arnold. It's probably not what you expected."

The other one shook my hand and said, "Welcome. I'm Rick. I do all the other stuff these two don't do. We're all certified to pilot this craft in case of emergencies, so don't worry, and if we all perish, the ground control can bring it back with computers, or we are actually capable of making a jump to a nearby base of ours in a close star system. Only needed to do that once, and it worked."

"I don't know whether I feel better or worse," I said, and they all laughed.

Milo motioned me to a seat, and the auto belts secured me. As soon as everyone was seated, the screens came on, and it looked as if we had opened the windows. The hangar door opened, and it led into another smaller hangar slightly larger than the craft, and then it closed behind us. The outer door slowly opened, and water roared in and came up and around the windows. Small jellyfish-like creatures floated in the water. After exiting the hangar into the dark ocean, we started rising slowly out of the water and then into the air. Stretch was pressing various places on the consoles, and everyone else seemed to be just enjoying the ride.

The ocean was beautiful from there, and I could see several boats going in different directions. It was amazing how many ships were on the ocean at any given time. Some islands stood out because they were lit up. Several airplanes were going different directions. I almost forgot how excited I was that we were going to the moon and maybe Mars. Soon we were in low Earth orbit, going toward the North Pole. The earth was round from that vantage point, and soon we were over the North Pole. We stopped, and Stretch said, "Watch this—look at the outside monitors."

All of a sudden, there was lightning over the whole outside of the ship. This happened for about thirty seconds.

"That was sterilizing the outside, and we come over the poles, so it will just look like the aurora borealis if anyone were to see it," Captain Stretch said. "We have to stop on our return and do the same thing, plus we'll do it when we leave the moon and Mars."

"How long of a voyage is it to the moon?" I asked.

"We could be there in a few seconds if need be, but we like to take our time and look at things," said Captain Arnold. "We'll take about thirty minutes, and you won't be bored with the scenery."

I could feel the craft speed up. In about a minute, the seat belts retracted and everyone got up and started moving around. I walked around to the different monitors and windows, and behind me, I could see the earth slowly getting smaller. *It sure is beautiful,* I thought.

I could not believe how many stars were visible. I had to remember that many of those stars were actually galaxies like the Milky Way, with billions of stars themselves.

All of a sudden, there was music coming from everywhere, and the song was "Everyone's Gone to the Moon" by Jonathan King from the sixties. Then there was "Blue Moon" by the Marcels, the slow version, followed by Van Morrison's "Moon Dance." Then we heard "Moon Shadow" by Cat Stevens and "Blue Moon of Kentucky" by Ricky Skaggs and John Fogerty. By then, I was ready for another heavenly body of some type, but the music died down, and the moon was very large in front of us.

We stopped on the dark side and sterilized again. Then we slowly descended to the surface and around to the lighted side. From the window, I could see the American flag left there. It was partially shredded, probably from small meteorites, I would imagine.

Milo said, "Time to get suited up." I followed him into a small room, and there were suits a lot like the NASA crew had worn, but the backpacks were different. They were smaller, and the material appeared to be more flexible. "Last chance for the restroom before our adventure," said Milo, pointing to a cabin-like place. I went in, and when I emerged, Milo was already getting into his suit. Captain Rick was getting into one also, but the other two Vesi were not. I took the suit and put my feet in first, and then I pulled it on and pushed my arms into the gloves.

"These gloves feel like leather," I said. "Very easy to move in."

"Yes, and protective. These will stop most small meteorites without any damage except maybe a bruise. Our ship will keep us aware if there are any larger ones getting close," said Milo. "Put on your helmet and let's get a checkout. The suit will check itself and report to the ship. It will take a few minutes until you get used to the moon's gravity. The ship's artificial gravity matched the earth's most of the trip but it slowly started matching the moon's when we got closer. You will still have to adjust once we're on the surface. Oh, and you can take a moon rock back as a souvenir if you like, even though they're just like rocks on Earth. It will get sterilized before it reenters."

We walked into a room about the size of an elevator, and the door behind us closed. After all the suit checks were completed, I could hear air escaping, and then the lights went down and back up, and I knew this time we were getting sanitized. The outside door opened, and a small ladder was extended to the surface. As I walked out, I could see that it was covered with a dust layer, but the gravity sure made me feel light. It was like walking on a trampoline except it didn't sink down. I looked around, and it was just like all the pictures I had seen of the moon. I saw some junk that NASA had left behind years earlier, like the descent stage of Apollo 11. After I'd walked around for a while and gotten my "moon legs," Milo asked me if there was anything I wanted to see or do.

"Yes. I'd like to find the golf balls Alan Shepard hit up here."

Milo said, "Did you copy, Stretch?"

"Working on it," was the reply. A moment later, I heard, "We'll have to go to the Apollo 14 site. Climb aboard and we can be there in a few minutes."

We got back in and sat down without unsuiting, and a few minutes later, we landed again and got back out.

After a few minutes of readjusting to the gravity, I was told to follow the dot on my space helmet. I noticed a dot that seemed to be on the surface of the helmet, staying pointed toward the target no matter which way I turned.

"Just put the locator in front and start walking. It will get larger the closer you get." I started looking at the dot, and it wasn't long before it started growing larger, and then it was almost completely covering the helmet.

"It is in the dust within three feet of where you are standing," Stretch said. I started moving the dust, and there was one of them. The ball looked as if it had been there for a while. It was dirty but in no worse shape than any other found golf ball.

"Okay, let's get the other one," I heard, and another dot showed up on my helmet at the side. I turned so it was in front of me and started walking. I stepped on something and looked down. It was a staff off some equipment.

"What the hell is this?" I asked.

"That was tossed like a javelin by Astronaut Mitchell on one of the trips. Do you want it?"

"No, just the golf balls," I replied. Within a few minutes, I had picked up the other one also. I put them in one of the pockets on my suit. I looked around. *Beautiful desolation*, I thought. No wind, no life, not much of anything, but it was beautiful in a different sort of way. There were desolate places on earth but not like this. There was no sky, and the horizon was closer. Wherever you looked were just rock, dust, and craters. It would have been overwhelming had I not already known about the astronauts and what they had done and seen there. I was wondering why humans would spend so much money to return here, unless we discovered some reason like mining or something. It would make a good observatory, but the space station was probably as good—and a lot closer to earth.

After I had looked around for what was probably a couple of hours, Milo asked if I wanted to see anything else. I said there wasn't, asking if we could just take a surface tour on our way out. He said it wouldn't be a problem. We went back to the ship and headed inside. The door closed, and the sanitizers returned for a few seconds. The air came back into the room, and a beep in the helmet signaled that it was safe to remove it. We removed our helmets and walked into the other room to get out of our suits. I remembered to get the golf balls out, and I put them in a little storage compartment there. I wasn't sure what I would do with them, but for some weird reason, I wanted them.

Everyone but me got busy doing this and that, and we all took our seats and got buckled in. We lifted off the surface about fifty feet or so. We took a slow ride across the surface, and I noticed for the first time that the craft wasn't stirring up any dust. We visited several sites where there was space debris left by the United States and Russia. There had actually been a lot of debris on the moon, but I supposed it really wasn't hurting much. We went to some of the better known places and finally started lifting off. Once we were in a higher orbit, we stopped and sanitized the craft, and then we started toward open space.

Captain Rick took out some sandwich-like things and water for us all, and before I could ask, Stretch said it would take about an hour and half to get to Mars. We were moving quite fast by Earth standards, but not by space standards. She explained that we had to go a little slower than we were actually capable of because we had a magnetic shield that was used to deflect some of the small meteorites. If we went too fast and the meteorite was meeting us at a high speed, the shield wouldn't work. We would just have to avoid any large meteorites or space debris. Speaking of the latter, it was amazing how much space junk there was around the earth itself compared to the small amount out there.

In a way, I was glad there weren't many Mars songs, and Stretch asked if I'd like engine noise. I said I was okay without it now, so she just put on some classical music softly in the background. I was still amazed at the number of stars, galaxies, and things I could see, and then I realized that I was not seeing 90 percent of the stuff in space, commonly referred to as dark matter and dark energy.

I sat back and stared at the Milky Way, completely awed by the number of stars and the order there seemed to be to the galaxy. And then I realized that the earth was out in the "burbs" of the Milky Way, so to speak. What a trip. Looking out the window, I actually nodded off for a while. All of a sudden, I woke up and saw Mars in front of us, getting larger, and I started getting anxious. No other Earthling that I knew of had been there. I reminded myself to ask about that later on. We were slowing, and the adrenaline was starting to increase, so I started sitting up, looking closer at Mars.

We stopped and sanitized as usual before slowly descending to the surface. It looked dry, rocky, and reddish. It could have been any desert in the western

United States, except that it didn't have any vegetation that I could see. Then someone said, "Look out there" and pointed to a window. I looked, and there were about thirty creatures looking like the grays. They were holding a large sign that read "Yankees, go home" and another that read "Mars is for Martians." At first, I thought it was real, and then everyone started laughing. It had been inserted into the screen display. Still, it was funny.

It was time to get back into the suits. We were using the same ones that we had worn on the moon, but the tanks had been changed. We went through the same procedures, and when we stepped out, the gravity was a lot higher than on the moon but still less than half that on Earth. I looked around and asked where we were. Within a few seconds, a map of Mars was on my helmet, and I could see that we were almost at the Martian equator. It appeared that there used to be a lot of running water on the surface. I bent down and checked to see if it was dusty like the moon. It was dusty, but not as bad as the moon. There were many small rocks and pebbles and some larger ones also. I picked up some rocks and looked closely at them. They were a reddish brown. I assumed this was from high iron content. Usually it is.

I asked Milo if there was any form of life here, and he said there was down below the surface in most places, but we would visit the poles that had more water. I asked him if we were going to see the rovers. He said we would fly over them, but we wouldn't take a chance on them photographing us. We walked around, picked up rocks, and put them back. I soon realized that the only reason to go to Mars would be to see if life was anywhere else in the solar system—or universe, for that matter. I had the answer to that already, and I could only think that instead of manned flights, why didn't we just send rovers to take a core sample and surface samples from different places, returning them to the space station for analysis? That seemed cheap compared to a manned mission.

After looking around for about an hour, I was ready to go someplace else. We got back in the craft but kept our suits on; we still had to go through the sanitizing procedure. We then went over to see Olympic Mons.

"Good grief, that's impressive," I said.

"Yes, it is. I don't think I would want to be close if it went active again," said Arnold.

It was so big that it had to be observed from orbit to see the whole thing. It was about the size of Arizona. From the ground, we would not have been able to see it all at once, due to the curvature of the planet. We made a circle around the volcano, and I realized just how big it was.

When everyone seemed satisfied, we continued on to the polar region, where there was ice. We landed and went out to the surface again. There was a type of moss-looking stuff growing there. I played with it for a while and was surprised how thrilled I was. It no longer mattered to me that there was life on Mars since I already knew there were all types of life around the galaxy and the universe. In a way, the fact that there was not much life outside the earth in our own solar system was a relief to me. The way we are able to conduct wars on Earth, how would it be if we had a competing planet? I could just see the headlines now: *Earth to liberate Mars from terrorists. President says it is better to fight them there than here on Earth.* I figured that moss would be safe for a few years.

I was surprised that after about eight hours, I was actually ready to go back toward Earth. We went through the sanitizing procedures, and I did bring back a small rock as a souvenir. It went through the sanitizer also. On the trip back, we stopped by the two moons Deimos and Phobos, but we didn't get out. Deimos is only about nine miles across and is probably just a captured meteorite, while Phobos is about sixteen miles long, and was probably also captured, with a dust covering about three feet thick. As they say, "Nothing to see here."

It was a good trip back, and I noticed the amount of stuff orbiting the Earth. Any civilization can easily find out if there's life on Earth by just looking at all the stuff orbiting around it. We stopped and sanitized before we reentered the atmosphere. We slowly descended down to a few thousand feet and took a tour of the eastern seaboard on our way back to the Puerto Rican Trench and home. I had no idea what time it was. It was dark, so we just eased back into the water and down to the base. We entered the hangar, and Milo and I went back through the sanitizer. Stretch and the others were busy doing stuff on the ship to secure it—or whatever they had to do to finish a mission.

Milo said we would get a few hours of sleep, and then we would decide what was next. I went to my room and took a shower, but while I was in it, I realized how stupid it was to take a shower after I had just gone through the sanitizer several times.

I wondered if other civilizations might be more advanced than the Vesi, having transporters and stuff like that. Then I asked myself how in the hell anyone could be more advanced than the Vesi, but then I remembered that I'd thought humans were really advanced a couple of weeks ago. I didn't want to think about all this stuff right now. I lay down and dropped off to sleep.

When I woke up, I saw that it had only been a couple of hours, but I was totally refreshed. I wondered what was left to see, but I was never disappointed. In a few minutes, Milo came around, and we went to get something to eat. We had a light meal of soup and sandwiches. Milo asked if there was something I would like to do or see, and I thought for a minute.

"What about the birth of Christianity?" I responded.

"That's possible, but I believe you might want to wait until you have a lot of time for that one," Milo said. "Something like a week's vacation or so because you are going to want to see a lot of that story."

I agreed because I wouldn't know exactly where to start, and there was much of the story that I had questions about. "Can we go see some of your labs?" I asked.

"Sure," Milo said. "I know one thing I wanted to show you earlier." He motioned for me to follow him, and off we went. We went to Medical Lab 17. The sign changed into English as we approached. Inside, it looked like most normal labs topside, but I didn't know what many of the instruments were. Milo walked over and picked up something that looked like the screen to a laptop computer. I did not see any keyboard or input device, but Milo pressed the corner, and it sprang to life.

Milo said, "This is handy for finding out what is going on inside the body. It works on several different types of sensors, and none of the emissions are harmful to any type of life. It uses more passive than active sensors. Put your hand out on the table."

I did so, and he placed the thing over my hand. With a few movements of his fingers, I could plainly see all the bones as if they were right there. They looked like holographs, and when I moved them around, I didn't feel anything out of the ordinary.

Milo said, "Watch this." He slid his finger up the side. I could now see the muscles in my hand as plain as day. I could also watch them work. Then it changed, and I could see all the blood vessels and then the nerves. There was a zoom feature, and Milo could zoom in on one nerve and watch it as if it were under a microscope.

"This can be adjusted to specific types of cells, based on density and some other things, or to a certain distance, making the view look like a slice of the organ. Or combinations of these so you can see anything in the body. It makes research and diagnosis much simpler. This is a portable unit. We have some that are more complex, for use in what humans refer to as a clinic or hospital, but most all of their work is for accidents since we have very few other medical problems."

I didn't know what to say, but I sure wished I had one. I could make a mint, but then I was still thinking like a capitalistic human, not that there was anything wrong with that. Just think how this could be used at airport security. Then again, if everyone were like the Vesi, we wouldn't need airport security. I was sure there were some bad sides to the Vesi, but it could just also be human mistrust based on thousands of years of being "civilized."

Milo said, "We have a DNA reader that can make instant readings, and it will tell who the owner is instantly. It takes a lot of the work out of the labs. They could be doing something beneficial instead of solving crimes that should never have been committed in the first place. That's going to require many changes in society, but I fear you are a long way from that, if ever.

"You've seen some of our microscopes—or rather, nano and pico scopes— and you should spend some time with them," Milo said. "The atom is such an exciting thing once you see what it's really like. Once you study the chains, it will start—and I mean *start*—to make sense. What else would you like to see?"

"You know, I'm starting to feel exhausted, and I think I'll hold my questions until a later time. After all, I've have been to the moon and Mars, and that was tiring. I think I'll return and absorb what's happened. When do we talk about this mission I'm supposed to be on?"

"This week I will be topside and bring some Kobe steaks. We'll discuss it then. It won't take long, and it will be an easy decision for you, I think," said Milo.

With that, we went out to the small hangar and went topside, where it was dark. The craft dropped me off near the parking lot of the airport. There was a shuttle bus stop just a few yards away, and I caught the bus after about five minutes. It took me to my car, and I was home shortly. I was indeed tired, and the animals were glad to see me. They quickly settled back down and came in to sleep with me. All was well in the world at that moment.

Soon I was extremely sleepy, but I knew I would be doing replays in my head for a while. I couldn't believe that I had been to the moon and Mars. I thought about how everyone on Earth should do that, given the opportunity. Then another thought shot forward: *How many humans have taken that trip, and did they feel the way I did?* More questions to ask. Every answer I'd received only brought more questions. It was possible I had reached my full capacity for thinking. *Oh, what the hell,* I kept telling myself. *My brain will stop when it gets full.*

Chapter Eleven: The Mission

Monday at school was fairly normal for somebody who had been to the moon and Mars over the weekend. Just another routine weekend off, right? I couldn't wait to find out what this so-called mission of mine was. Monday evening, Troy came over to my house all excited.

"Guess what happened!" Troy said. After my weekend, I couldn't imagine anything more exciting.

"You won the lottery?" I asked.

"Pretty close! I have an opportunity for my own real estate office out in Washington State!" he said. "The only problem is that I have to decide right now, but since it is what Linda and I have always wanted, we're going to do it."

"That's wonderful," I said. "I'll miss you guys, but opportunity usually doesn't return if you don't hear the knock."

"I know, but it won't be the same," he said.

I hated to see them go since they were such good neighbors. But I knew it was a dream come true, so I was happy for them. They had a moving company there on Tuesday, and everything was gone in a flash. I guess the company that had hired him had bought his house, so there wasn't any problem with the move.

Milo called and said he would come Wednesday evening for our talk. When Wednesday arrived, I stopped at the store on the way home to get a few things for the cookout. Lo and behold, at the checkout stand, on one of the tabloids, was a story about an alien abduction of three good ol' boys in Georgia. It read *Aliens abduct and molest local boys. Sheriff says alcohol may be involved.* I almost laughed aloud, but I did buy one.

When Milo arrived, he gave me a couple of Kobe beef steaks and a bottle of Lafite-Rothschild wine. I opened it, and we chatted about the wine for a few minutes. I started fixing the steaks and wondered aloud how I would mess them up, but Milo said he doubted that I could do that. We had our dinner, and Ralph got some scraps, which he didn't seem to appreciate any more than usual, but then again, he was not a snooty dog.

After dinner, Milo gave me a good cigar and asked what Troy was doing. "Do I need to leave some for him?" he inquired.

"Funny thing you should ask," I said. "Troy and Linda moved to the Northwest suddenly this week. He said he would let me know what was going on as soon as they got settled."

Milo said, "I know you liked them a lot, but you'll never hear from them again," he said.

"What? They're very nice," I replied with some irritation. "I think they'll keep in touch."

"Yes, they are, but I have some inside information. No, nothing bad has happened to them, but their mission here was finished so they moved on," he added.

I stopped mid-puff and stared at Milo. "Mission?" I asked. "Were they …?"

Milo replied, "Yes, they were Vesi, and they were the ones who recommended you for contact. You see, we don't do many things in haste, especially by Earth time. They recommended you for a mission, and their part was accomplished, so they went on to another mission."

I was totally stunned. For a moment, I felt betrayed, then surprised, and then amazed and confused. "What's my mission?" I asked.

"It's so simple that you might not believe it. We want you to write a book and tell everything that has happened to you so far … and don't leave out anything," Milo said.

"You are joking, of course," I said.

"This time I'm not," Milo said seriously.

"No one is going to believe it," I said.

"We know," Milo answered. "First of all, it is doubtful that you will even be able to get it published. You would be an unknown author, and the story would be too science fiction. Very few publishers would even bother to read it, much less publish it.

"Second, on the off chance that some minor publisher might pick it up, very few people would buy it and read it. Even fewer would believe any of it. So, all things considered, less than one-tenth of one percent of people might actually think it could or did happen."

He continued, "Of that group, only a few people might get an idea that something could possibly be produced and actually work on it. You see, we don't think short-term about anything. We've had long discussions about whether this is aiding the advancement of humans. We discussed whether this might be against our principles and decided that the small possibility that some human might think some of these ideas are good, or that the technology might be possible and start work, is so small that statistically it's not significant enough to really affect any change. You see, we have actually gotten fond of humans, and we would like to see them advance, but we are concerned that they are heading in the wrong directions in some areas."

"I don't know how to write," I said. "I've never written anything except papers for college classes."

"Not a problem," Milo said. "That's even better because it will look as if it's coming from a rank amateur. If we had wanted it published for sure, we would have picked a known published author who would have gotten it published whether or not it was any good. In exchange, you can come down and visit whenever you like and see the history videos of any period. You'll have free access to any of the technology we use while downside. Besides, we have a few more travels in mind for you. You might even have follow-up books to write if you beat the odds and are actually published. Even if you don't, you will have a beautiful rejection form letter suitable for framing." Milo laughed.

This was going to be difficult. I thought for a while as I sipped my after-dinner brandy and smoked a wonderful cigar. I didn't know how to write a book, but then again, it was almost like writing a diary. There would be professionals to correct it and blah, blah, blah. After maybe three minutes of internal wrangling, it came out almost as if I didn't have any control: "You've got a deal, and when do I start?" I said.

"Whenever you'd like. Remember, we are in no hurry. So don't feel rushed," Milo said. "Anytime you have any questions, feel free to ask. Nothing you have seen so far is off limits. It is best to tell it as you saw it. The more truthful you are, the less believable you will be to the average human. But we are not interested in getting to the average human. We want to get to that one in a billion nonaverage human who might look at it and actually be in a position to do something."

We talked for a while, and then Milo left. I didn't know if I could do this or not. I did know that I couldn't resist seeing some of the holographic videos. I had just touched the surface. I hadn't even scratched it yet. I knew that the rest of my life would involve finding answers to things I had wondered about. Seeing other planets and galaxies would be so interesting. I just wished Karol was here to share this, but I'm not sure I would have been selected if she were. I knew that in the future, I also would be looking at everyone and wondering if he or she was Vesi. The future looked busy, and I hoped I was ready.

I thought about things for a while. I hadn't known why I wanted the golf balls from the moon, but it seemed I had to have them. After looking at them for a few weeks, I thought I should return them to their rightful owner. Alan Shepard Jr. had passed away, but he had two daughters. I packaged the balls up individually and found where they lived. This took some detective work, but I located them and sent them anonymously to them. I would have loved to be there when they opened them.

In each package, I had included a handwritten note: *I think your father lost this, and I'm sure he would want you to have it. I'll be disappointed if I see it on eBay in a few years.*

Chapter Twelve: The Planets and Beyond

It had been several weeks since I'd spoken to Milo, and I was just letting things soak in and trying to think how I could I possibly write a book. I knew nothing about writing, other than research papers, and I wasn't that good with them. But I did always get an A or B because I was good with the facts. I was also thinking about how it would be to travel out of the solar system. Was it possible? All the things I had seen in the past few weeks were still hardly believable, and I thought how many scientists would be wild to see 1 percent of it. I had been to the moon, and only several humans had ever done that. And I had been to Mars, whereas no humans had been acknowledged for going there. I then started to wonder how many other Earthlings had been invited to this "inner circle," or whether the whole thing was an elaborate scam. I gave up on the idea of a scam.

I decided to give Milo a call and see how things were going. He assured me there was no way my phone could be tapped when I called him because it had been fixed, and actually, the phone company couldn't even tell I was making a call. I talked to him, asking if it would be possible to go out of the solar system. He said it was no problem, but we need more time. The Christmas vacation was coming up, and he said that would be perfect. I needed to get somebody to take care of the animals, however.

I asked the other teachers at school, and several recommended the same people, so I figured they were good. I made arrangements and called Milo, asking him if I needed to bring anything, and he said the only two things I needed were an open mind and a vivid imagination. I assured him I would bring both along. I started getting worried about something going wrong. But then, this wasn't like when the Apollo astronauts went to the moon. They were lucky to get back with the technology of the day. They were lucky to get into orbit much less to the moon, land on it, walk on it, return, and land safely.

How brave and dedicated those men and women had been to accomplish that. If all of humanity were like them, well we would probably be ... well, Vesi. I think I was starting to take baby steps to understanding life in the universe.

The day finally came when school was out for a couple of weeks, and I was about to experience something that I had not the foggiest idea about. Milo said it would be a custom-built cook's tour. I wasn't sure what he meant but figured it would be like a sampler platter with a little of this and some of that. Milo said he would pick me up at my house since the neighbors had seen him there several times—nobody would think anything of it.

When Milo arrived, I went out with a suitcase in case some of the neighbors were watching.

"Hello, Milo," I said.

"Hello, Mac," he replied. "Are you ready for a sojourn?"

"I think I am," I replied.

"I've got a special bonus for you," he said. "We will sometimes be traveling for a full day or longer, and so you don't get bored looking at stars and galaxies and stuff, you might want to pick some time recordings to take along with you. We have a holograph projection room—smaller, of course, than the one at central—in which you can entertain yourself."

"That would be great," I said. "I've always wanted to know what was actually said and thought during the Continental Congress and at other times."

"Well, we don't know what they were thinking, but we can show you what they were saying," Milo said.

"That brings up an interesting question," I said. "Haven't the Vesi been able to do mind reading and thought transmissions and all that stuff?"

"This might sound crazy, but as capable as our technology is, we still cannot read thoughts. We can make muscles move by thinking about them and so forth, but the brain is organized in a way that is difficult to read from person to person ... or from Vesi to Vesi. We can read emotions such as anger, but we can't tell why you are mad. When I say we can read, I don't mean as individuals, but with our instruments," he continued.

It was starting to get dark, and we went to a large parking lot near the airport and parked. We waited until it got dark and the ship or craft or whatever it was showed up, and then we were off in no time. I am still amazed how black and silent those things were. I guess radar just ignored them, and that was fine with me. It was amazing how most UFO sightings report that they have lights on them. That's because humans are used to airplanes and copters having lights. If I were a UFO, I wouldn't have lights either, unless I wanted to be seen. I have always wondered about that, and I'm skeptical of any UFO that involves lights and noise, with the exception of the time we took the good ol' boys for a ride.

We went out into the Atlantic and slowly entered the water, leaving a small wake that dissipated in no time. We went down into the command center in the side of the trench. It still impressed me how they did this so cleanly and dryly. Milo suggested we get something to eat before we left because we would be eating things like MREs (meals ready to eat), as soldiers have to in battle.

I asked, "Can we get Sam to get us something?"

"Great idea," said Milo, and we headed up to the level were Sam would be. Milo went over to the box and said into it, "Sam, are you in range?"

"Be there in about five minutes," came out of the box.

Milo and I talked a little about how smart dolphins really are, and I found out that some of the whales are just as smart but more independent. Surprisingly, whales and dolphins rarely communicate. They can understand each other somewhat, but they have two entirely different structured languages. Sounds like humans. I was wondering if Sam ever knew any of the dolphins that were in places like Sea World and so forth.

In a few minutes, Sam was at the window, and he said, "Hello, Milo. Hello, walker. Let's see, your name is Mac or something like that, right?"

"Right," I said.

"Would you like some fresh seafood tonight, gentlemen?" he asked. "And I use the term lightly." He grinned.

"What would you like?" Milo asked.

"What about a flounder?" I replied.

"A five pounder like before?" Sam asked.

"That would be great," Milo said.

Sam took off like a bullet, saying he would drop it off and it would go straight to the kitchen.

Milo and I left, going to what I would consider a library. We went to a terminal, for lack of a better name, and he told me to put in the dates I would like to see ... and the general area of the world. I entered Philadelphia and the years from the 1770s. I also picked the years 50 BC to 50 AD and the area of Israel. The Vesi didn't use the designation BC and AD, but for human convenience they used the Gregorian calendar. In a couple of seconds, a small door beside the terminal opened, and a couple of shiny cubes emerged with Vesi language on them. The writing did not change to English for me, and I assumed it was because it was only printing. Milo said not to worry because he could tell which was which when the time came.

We then went to the restaurant and the maitre d' directed us to our seats and asked if we wanted drinks. I ordered a scotch and water, and Milo got a

Manhattan. He never seemed to order the same thing twice. This amused me for some reason. Our salads arrived quickly, and yet again, I couldn't believe the quality of the food. *If I'd had a place like this on the surface …* And then I realized I was thinking like a human again. I had to break that habit. Not that there's anything wrong with being a human. I had an internal laugh and thought how lucky I was.

We finished dinner, and Milo asked if I was ready to go. We walked to the hangar area, going in a different door than we had before. Inside were a couple of the ships that looked just like the others, except these were much larger and had antennae or something around the tops of them, bending back over the craft. We went over to the one with the open door and went inside. There were three Vesi inside. They looked like normal people as they busily checked gauges and pushed buttons. There were two males and a female. Their uniforms, or whatever they were, bore some kind of insignia that was Greek to me.

Milo said, "Hello crew. This is Mac, our newest guest." They all said hello and nodded. I was the center of attention as they introduced themselves.

"Hello, I'm Fran. I'm the flight commander, or star master, as we call it, but that sounds a little uppity to me since I can't master stars," she said. She was attractive but not a knockout, if you know what I mean. She looked all business, albeit friendly business. She was tall, thin, and physically fit.

"Hello, I'm Crash. Actually, it's Craig, but my nickname is Crash. Don't worry. It's only because of the way I play racing games. I take many chances, and most of them don't work out in the games. I'm a lot different here. I've never had an accident, and if we used wood, I would knock on it." He was a little younger but seemed equally assured of himself. He looked in great shape also. Military type.

"Hello, they call me Arrow, but my name is Aaron," he said. "Like an arrow, I can find the shortest and straightest distance between any two points of almost any navigator." He looked like a bit of a nerdy type. *Probably great in math and science,* I told myself.

"Do you have a nickname, Fran?" I asked.

Everyone laughed, and she said, "Behind my back, they call me Fran the führer. But that's just because I take my job seriously, and no one gets hurt if they vill just comply vith my orders. You understand?"

Everyone laughed, and I wasn't sure I was supposed to, but I did as well.

"You vill have a good time, understood?" she said.

"*Jawohl,*" I said, and everyone laughed. She did look as if she could be German. *Ah! Very interesting*, I said to myself.

Crash showed me to the place to change clothes, and they had a uniform for me, but there were no Depends this time, so I assumed we would be traveling for a good bit of time before we needed to get ready. I, of course, went through the sterilizer after I had changed.

"Are you ready for this?" Milo asked.

"Yes, I am," I said, sounding, I'm sure, like a ten-year-old going to Disney World.

Milo motioned to an awaiting seat, and as usual, it fit itself to me and secured me. Every car on Earth needed to have seats like that.

"Last chance to back out," said Milo.

"In for a penny, in for a pound," I answered.

"All right, it's a go, Fran," Milo said.

"And away we go," she replied.

Fran started pushing controls and moving the joystick. We moved slowly into another room, large enough for the craft, and the doors closed behind us. The water started coming in, but it took a little longer since this was a larger craft. After a while, the room was filled, and the other side opened into the sea. We slowly went out into the ocean and proceeded out for a short distance. We were going rather slowly, and I guess I looked concerned, because Fran turned and said to me, "You look worried, but we're going slowly because there is a submarine fairly close, and in spite of our ability to ignore radar, we can still be detected by some of the newer sonar equipment. If we go slowly, our hull will send back signals that make us look like a whale or school of fish until we are well out of their range."

We traveled like this for maybe five minutes, and then we started speeding up a little. We also started ascending toward the surface, and in a few minutes, we were out of the water and headed upward. I was still amazed. When we left the atmosphere, we stopped and went through sterilization of the ship. This took a little longer since this craft was larger.

"Where are we headed?" I asked.

Arrow answered, "We are heading out toward the gas planets, and we will drive by the ones that are presently on this side of the sun, but we'll catch the others on the return trip because we'll be returning from the opposite direction."

"Sounds like a plan, I think," I replied.

I could see in one of the viewers the planet of Jupiter. It was fairly small in the viewer, but I could make out which one it was. We started moving. Although I could barely feel it, I could tell we were going faster and faster.

Fran said, "You'll feel a little heavier for a few seconds as our ship's gravity system adjusts to the speed. Everything will be back normal as soon as it's synchronized."

I did start to feel heavier, but it was not uncomfortable or painful or anything. I thought the stars would go streaking by like in the movies, but in reality, I hardly noticed any change, except that Jupiter was getting bigger fast, and we did go past several asteroids in the asteroid belt. We didn't appear to be in any danger from them, but I wouldn't want to hear that some of the bigger ones were heading toward Earth.

After twenty minutes or so, we started slowing down, and Jupiter was enormous in the viewer. Since we were under the pull of Jupiter, I got a slight feel of the ship pulling backward to assist in slowing down. We were inside the orbits of the Jovian moons. The moons themselves were quite remarkable, and we visited each of the largest Galilean moons for about five minutes each. At this distance, you could also make out the rings of Jupiter. There were many minor moons looking like everything from dwarf planets to tumbling potatoes. The major Galilean moons—Io, Europa, Ganymede, and Callisto—all have their own personalities and sound so romantic. Then I remembered that they were just large rocks. Europa looked exciting. I asked if there was any life there.

Fran said, "There is, but the most advanced are like jellyfish. They would fit in on Earth, but they aren't very advanced. It's too cold for most creatures, although there is some warm water down deep that keeps rising and cooling. We made a lap around the planet and took a good look at it. It was quite impressive—about thirteen hundred times larger than Earth. Think of a pea compared to a grapefruit. It was extremely colorful, with mostly whites, reds, browns, and oranges—and ironically, those are considered earth tones on Earth.

It was time to head out again, and I could feel the ship picking up speed and weight. We headed to Saturn, and in the viewer was a small pinpoint in the center of the viewer. The aft viewer showed Jupiter getting smaller, and it was still fascinating.

"Fran, how fast are we traveling?" I asked.

"Watch this indicator," she replied, touching what looked like a thermometer. When she touched it, the panel turned to English and became a speedometer, for lack of a better word. It had RVSPE on it.

"What does that mean?" I asked.

She said, "Relative Velocity to a Static Point on Earth, or RELVEL for short."

She went on, "Since time and speed and distance and weight are all interrelated, the best way to have a relative indication of speed is to reference it to a point on Earth that doesn't move. If you were standing there looking at the ship, it would appear to be moving at that speed."

It also had a digital readout, and I noticed about the number 99.99932.

When we started slowing down, the digits started dropping fast and finally changed to kilometers per second, and then per minute, and then per hour.

"Do Vesi use the metric system?" I asked.

"We adapted to it since everyone on Earth, except the Americans, uses it. We had a similar system, but it was based on one diameter of our home planet that was no longer there. It turned out to be easily convertible to the metric system."

The Saturn rings were much more pronounced than the rings of Jupiter—and more colorful. We went by them slowly, relatively speaking, and they were all different. Just beautiful! Rocks, ice, crystals, and other stuff.

All the gas giants were beautiful just for their colors and swirling features. For creatures like humans and Vesi, living on them was out of the question, however. We looked at the moons of Saturn. Saturn has many moons, but most of them are small. Titan, however, was large and had an atmosphere. It also had a watery layer underneath, and I wondered if it had any type of life.

I asked, "Is there any life on Titan?"

Fran replied, "Yes, but it is microscopic. There are several chemophiles living there. Not very evolved and not very interesting by space standards, but the humans would love to find out about them."

"Yes, we would," I said.

We started accelerating again, and I knew we were on to the next planet. I assumed we were going to Uranus. I asked if that was the case.

Fran replied, "Actually, no. Uranus is on the other side of the sun at this time, and maybe we'll see it on the way back, but Neptune is close enough on this side. Actually, if you've seen Neptune, it is just like Uranus, except for some internal differences. They look an awful lot alike."

I just rested on that leg of the journey and enjoyed some space scenery. It was so vast and somewhat desolate, but that made it beautiful. We were there in what seemed like a few minutes, but I'm sure it was longer. It was a lovely blue planet but not at all like Earth. The moons were beautiful but after all the moons I had seen, they were fairly routine. I asked if we would be going by Pluto, and I was told that we would probably swing by it on our way back in.

Chapter Thirteen: First Jump

"Are you ready to leave the solar system?" Fran asked.

"I suppose so," I answered.

Fran said, "Just sit back and observe. This will not hurt, and we cannot fully explain how it happens. It was discovered by accident, and we just use it. We have a fairly extensive mapping of some parts of the universe."

Milo had been quiet, and I wondered why. I felt he was observing my reactions to what was going on, and I guessed that this was part of my evaluation or whatever.

We were going faster than we ever had, and I was watching the RELVEL meter, noticing that it had changed from speed of light to universe transit scale. This was on a scale from one to infinity, and I assumed that it was equivalent to *Star Trek*'s warp speed. The RELVEL was indicating about 1.8 when all of a sudden, everything went totally white, then totally dark, and then stars reappeared. I had a strange feeling inside. Not pain ... by any means. It was more like the feeling you get when watching a scary movie and the bad guy jumps out. I wasn't prepared for it, so it felt strange. I would be ready next time.

"What happened?" I asked.

"We made, for a lack of a better word, a jump," said Fran. "We are now about a third of the way into the Milky Way, and we will be entering a solar system much like the sun's system."

I could see a star that was a lot larger than any of the other visible ones were. I assumed this was where we were going. We went by a planet a lot like Neptune and began slowing dramatically. In the viewer were two Earth-like planets. One was approximately three-fourths the size of the other, but they were on different sides of their sun. The outer one had more icecap than the inner one.

"Which one are we going to visit?" I asked.

"Both of them," she said. "They both have life, but it's different. There is fairly intelligent life on the outermost planet. They have limited technology and no space travel, but it's still very interesting."

"We have to update your translators for this planet. The intelligent life forms here are, for all practical purposes, insects. We call them Insecteriams, but they usually refer to themselves as Ises. They are almost as large as small humans, but there are some differences between them and insects on Earth. They have a type of lungs and several hearts. They stand upright most of the time and have two legs and four arms. They have small antennae, and their language is high pitched, which we can barely hear, so we use a type of hearing aid. We have translator boxes to talk to them, a lot like we use for the dolphins. They are friendly but have no desire for space travel. They live in what would be described as similar to the eighteen hundreds, with electricity and some modern conveniences."

Milo handed me a couple of earplugs, which I assumed were the translators. I put them into my ears and had no loss of hearing. He then handed me a necklace with something that looked almost like an iPod on it. I assumed this was the translator for me to talk to them. I put it around my neck.

"Testing, one, two, three. Did you hear that?" asked Milo.

"Yes," I replied. "It was in English, and it said, 'Testing, one, two, three.'"

"Take them out for a second," Milo said. "I'll show you what it actually was."

I removed them, and then I heard something like cricket sounds. That was amazing, but I didn't know why I was continually impressed—I felt as if I were in the future. I put them back in since they didn't affect my normal hearing.

We started into the atmosphere after sterilization, slowly coming to a landing on the surface.

"These people aren't scared of the ship or us?" I asked.

"Not in the least. They are content with their lives and have no desire for space travel—or most technology, for that matter. They just go about their business and leave everybody else alone. There is a type of mammal on the planet, but it has never advanced past the small rodent stage. Probably because the Insecteriams developed first. Under no circumstances call them the B-word, bugs, because bugs are one of the things they raise for food. And please refrain from swatting or squashing any type of life here, as most of life is highly respected. They have many different life forms, but no birds or reptiles. We think there are no birds because they never had reptiles to evolve into them. But they do have some insect types that build nests and lay their eggs like birds."

"Do we need space suits?" I asked.

"No," replied Milo. "This planet and the other one here are close enough to Earth's gas standards to not require them. Later, we will visit some places where they are required. You will notice a sulfur smell when we first get out, but you'll adapt to it quickly."

Milo said, "Please stand still and don't touch anything. We are going to do an internal sterilization of the ship to make sure we didn't bring them any guests. We have to do one when we leave also."

Fran said, "Ready, three … two … one … execute." We all raised our hands. I guess this was to ensure that no one was touching anything. I felt something like static electricity go over me for a few seconds, and then Fran said, "Complete." This was a different type of sanitation from the lights we used earlier. *Another question.*

The door opened. A faint smell of sulfur was in the air. We went outside, and I saw many of the locals milling around. They didn't seem to mind our being there. Some of them looked at us for a few seconds and then went on with their business. We walked a short distance and came to one of the Insecteriams, which was busy operating some kind of electronic equipment. It looked ancient but seemed to be working fine. This creature looked like a giant praying mantis. The arms and legs were sturdier and the neck was thicker than a like-sized praying mantis would have been on Earth. It was about five feet tall. It did not have any wings that I could see. The only clothing was a belt like a fanny pack, which I call it for lack of a better description.

"Hello, Zebo," Milo said.

"Hello, Milo," I heard the words but didn't see anyone's mouth moving. Zebo turned to look at Milo.

This was somewhat weird. I heard bugs—excuse me, insects—speaking English, but then again, I didn't know why I was surprised about anything. For a long time, I'd thought cell phones were amazing.

"How have you been?" asked Milo.

"Great, by all standards," said Zebo. Again, I didn't see mouths moving, but they didn't have lips as we do. "Are you going to be able to stay until the next feeding cycle?"

"Yes," Milo said. "It would be our pleasure to join you, if it's no trouble."

"None," said Zebo. "Why don't you look around for a while, and we'll meet at Feeder 4 at eighteen point five on your time scale."

"Fine," said Milo.

We walked away and started going down a street. The traffic consisted of small carts running on tracks made of three rails, looking somewhat like a roller coaster. The rails were rounded at the top instead of flat, as they are on Earth, but I'm sure there was a reason. I assumed these were electric, but I might be wrong. These cars had covers that could be raised in case of weather problems. The cars seemed to be independent, and there would be one, two, or any number of cars connected, but there wasn't anything that looked like an engine. Occasionally, there was a larger car with more creatures in it. They all seemed to be computer controlled, as there was no one driving. The buildings seemed to be some kind of stone-type material, and I couldn't see much lighting.

"Why is there so little lighting?" I asked Milo.

"The Insecteriams have excellent infrared vision, so they need little visible lighting," he told me.

We stopped in a few stores. I didn't see any labels that looked like descriptions or prices, but there were signs on the walls, with pictures of the items in the stores. The language looked like a handful of sticks that had been thrown together. It made Asian writing look plain. We saw a few Insecteriams in the stores, but there were very few of them in each place. Come to think of it, the whole city seemed to be sparsely populated. I would have expected insects to be quite prolific, but maybe they had learned to control the population in order to avoid outstripping their resources. Intelligence seemed to be better utilized elsewhere in the universe than it sometimes was on Earth.

Most of the products I saw in these stores did not make much sense to me, until I realized that they had totally different body shapes, hand shapes, and so forth. I could recognize a few things, such as cloth and tools and containers, but for the most part, they would not sell well on Earth. The one thing I recognized was the fanny pack–type thing that Zebo was wearing. Then it dawned on me that they didn't seem to wear any clothes except those.

We went into a communication center. There were several Insecteriams standing and working on what looked like computer terminals, but the keyboards were weird. A few others were sitting around a table-like thing with what looked like a birdbath in the center. They were talking and occasionally drinking out of a communal bowl. The liquid looked somewhat like tea. They all ignored us, but when Milo spoke to them, they stopped and all of them looked at us and said, "Welcome."

Then one of them asked us if we would like a drink of what they were drinking. Before I could say anything, Milo said we would love to share with them. I noticed they had small proboscises that unrolled when they drank, and I wondered how this was going to work. Then one of them walked over to a cabinet and came back with a couple of straws like those on Earth, except they were shiny metal. When they handed them to us, they made a noise that sounded to me like laughing. As they all watched, I dipped my straw into the stuff and took a sip. Crap! It tasted like a cross between putrefied skunk and leftover urine, or what I guessed those things would taste like. I noticed that Milo didn't take a drink but waited for my reaction. I acted as if it didn't bother me, but they all started laughing again, and one of them handed us inserts and showed us how to put them in the straws. I tried the stuff again, and it tasted like sweet tea. I asked what it was, and one of them said it was the blood of something. Then he got a picture of what I would best describe as a wasplike creature.

We thanked them and left, and I wondered if it would poison me. Milo said it would not, but it was possible for it to upset my stomach if I had too much. I told him there was no danger of me having too much of that. He laughed.

It was almost time for our meal with Zebo, so we started back toward the town center. We found a building that had a temporary number four hanging on the door, so we went in, and there were numerous Insecteriams in there, eating various weird-looking things. They were using a type of utensil that looked a lot like a knife and fork on one end, while the other end was made for their physiology. Milo walked over to a table where Zebo was, but I had no idea how he could tell it was him.

There were two there, and Zebo said, "This is my current mate, Zeba."

This was a lot like languages on Earth, with the word ending indicating whether it was the male or female form of the word. We sat down, which wasn't easy since the chairs were made for the way the Insecteriams bodies were built. There were no backs, and they were short, but we made them work. There was a birdbath at this table also, and Zebo laughed when he saw me look at it.

"This one has water in it," Zebo said, "but you will still need your drinkers." He made a hand gesture, and in a few seconds, a smaller Insecteriam came over with two of the metal straws for Milo and me. We talked about the stuff we had tried today. It was somewhat like coffee for them, but it would not go over very well at Starbucks.

The food came. It looked like a ring of round meat with a hole in the middle, like a doughnut only larger. It was the color of chicken, and I was betting it would, of course, taste like chicken. We were given utensils that were much like knives and forks, and we started eating. The dish tasted like a cross between roasted grains and bacon. It was actually quite good. We also had a mixed salad type of dish made of different green things; it resembled grass with a few leaves mixed in. It was a little bitter but came with a dressing that was quite sweet. I asked what the meat was, and they said it was a type of caterpillar, for lack of a better description. We talked about the food for a while, and then I asked Zebo why they had never developed space travel.

"We have no desire to go anywhere else," Zebo said. "We're very happy here. We do have a few Ises that study the stars and have learned a lot from visitors, but we just don't want to go anywhere else. We live about thirty years by Earth time, so we don't have much time to get bored. By the time we mature and reproduce, it is about time to die. We have extended our lifetimes by about five years, which is a large change by our standards."

"We could imagine living as long as Earthers, maybe, but never as long as the Vesi. They are so interested in knowledge that they need to live longer. We would be bored if we lived a long time after reproducing, and it would tax our resources as well. Now every Ise works and is part of the system. In case of injury, we are taken care of until our normal death time. There are few diseases, so we have limited medical care. We also have very few different life forms here, so the competition isn't as great. All things considered, we are quite happy where we are."

Milo said, "I hate to spoil the party, but we need to leave because we have a schedule and another planet in this system to see."

We thanked Zebo and Zeba and walked back to our craft. We went through our sterilization procedures and left the planet.

That was extremely interesting. The Insecteriams were a lot more alien than the Vesi, but that's because they were physically different. I was tired, and clearly Milo could tell.

"We need to get some rest before we land on the other planet," Milo said. "By the way, it's going to be different from this one." He urged me to take a short nap, and I readily obliged.

Chapter Fourteen: The Triads

I woke up after what I thought was fifteen minutes, but in reality, it was four hours. When I got back into the control room, I could see we were orbiting the planet. Actually, we were in a geosynchronous orbit, where we were sitting over one spot on the planet, as most satellites on Earth do. I was the last one up, and everyone was busy doing things that looked important—like getting ready to go downside.

Milo said, "The life forms on this planet are not what we would consider intelligent as of yet. They are in the caveman stage and do have rudimentary weapons. They have discovered fire and how to use it, but they are probably centuries away from metalworking. They are most unique, as you will find out. They aren't dangerous, but we don't contact them directly since that might influence their development. We can watch from a distance since we have installed sensors in some of their living spaces. They migrate a lot, but they seem to return to the same places over and over."

He continued, "We make the outside of the ship look like the sky from the bottom and sides. We can change the color of the ship to any color—just as a cuttlefish or an octopus does—because the outside has LED-type pixels all over it. We use it on Earth a lot when we are out in the daytime, which we try to avoid if possible. You have heard of UFO reports about craft just disappearing. This is how most of them do it. Your other visitors are mostly just scout ships with no living creatures inside, and that's one of the reasons they can make such fast moves."

We were now on the ground, and Milo said we would not need suits. The atmosphere was close enough, but the oxygen was a little low. It was like being about ten thousand feet on Earth, so unless we had to make a run for it, there shouldn't be any problem. Fran and the other crew came with us this time because they said these creatures were rare in the universe, and they enjoyed seeing them occasionally. She said that since they had been watching them, they had made some improvements in their weapons, mainly due to discovering flint, which can make a sharper edge. There were some changes in spears but nothing great.

After sterilizing, we left the ship and walked about five hundred meters up a small hill. The vegetation was very short where we were. It was like grass but more blue than green. In the distance, I could see what looked like trees. We stopped on top of the hill. In the valley on the other side was a group of "them." I was shocked.

The creatures were hominoid types with lots of hair, and they were about the size of average humans. The big difference was that they were triangular. That is, they had three legs, three arms, and three eyes spaced fairly equally on their heads. Their noses were tiny, with larger openings than human noses. They had three of these spaced equally between the eyes. They each had only one mouth. Watching them, it was apparent that each favored the side of his body with the mouth. I assumed that was the front. I noticed several smaller creatures that I thought were children. After observing them, though, I realized they were different creatures and were probably a type of pet.

Milo said, "We call them Triads. Guess you don't have to ask why. We have discovered that all the creatures on this planet are triangular, and their DNA is also a triple helix. Guess the original creature was, and everything followed."

I did not see any birds, but there were some weird insects that had several wings and flew more like helicopters than planes. The Triads were mobile and could go in all directions quite easily. If I had a few of these for the NFL, I could be rich. *Guess it's hard to stop being human no matter where we go,* I thought. Then I realized that if humans knew of the wonders in the rest of the universe, maybe we wouldn't be so self-centered and could get excited about something other than money.

Not far from them were some creatures that appeared to be mammals. They were busy pulling and eating grass. They had six legs and were the size of sheep or goats. Some of them had horns that were in a triangular shape opposite the mouth side of the head. They had hair, or fur, that looked like wool.

It was so fantastic that I wanted to know other humans who may have been there past and present. I was still wondering how many people on Earth were walking around with this knowledge and weren't able to discuss it with anybody. All of a sudden, it made me feel lonely, and I realized I could only discuss these things with the Vesi. What a bummer, in a way. I wondered if DaVinci, Galileo, or any other famous people had been privy to this—and if they did some of their wonderful things based on this knowledge. If you think people now would think I'm a nut, can you imagine what they would have thought of them back then? They didn't fare too well anyway, and their technology was primitive compared to ours, much less that of the Vesi. My head was starting to build up pressure again.

I looked back at the ship, and it was hard to see. It blended in with the surroundings, but if you looked closely, you could see a slight shimmer but nothing else. This technology sure would be great for the military, and then I realized that if we were more like the Vesi, we would not need a military.

We watched the Triads for several hours. They seemed to go about their business as usual. They had a campfire that they occasionally put more wood on, and they had some kind of rock that also burned. There were several piles of these around the site. There was a cave, or what looked like one, on the side of the next hill behind this group. They also had a place that they all went to when they had to use a bathroom. It was away from their camp and from the stream that ran through the floor of the valley. They were showing some signs of intelligence already. I was wondering how long it might be before they were buying houses they couldn't afford and selling derivatives that no one could explain. Then I realized that maybe there was hope for these creatures, and that they might be more Vesi-like than humanlike, and that might not be a bad thing.

It was nearly time to go, and in a way, I was disappointed that I couldn't watch these people develop, but then, it could be millions of years, if ever.

We got back in and eased off the planet, going through sterilization. I felt worse leaving there than I had leaving the Insecteriams because the Triads were more similar to mammals in structure, except for the extra limbs, eyes, etc. I felt as if I had been looking at Earth a few million years ago. I knew I could get the cubes and see what it was like, but seeing it in person was a lot more personal.

We started moving, and we were soon going rather fast. I looked at the RELVEL, which read 8.45. "How come we aren't jumping like before?" I asked.

Fran said, "Not only do you have to have the speed, but you have to be at the right place to jump. The first time it happened was a total surprise. After it happened, we stopped and went back through, learning that we could go back and forth with no harm. We started expanding out from there, and before long, we had a good group of jump points—or wormholes, as most humans dream about. Over the last few centuries, we have learned to figure out where they might be, and we can now predict with some accuracy where and at what speed we need to be to get to a certain point. This is how we learned to go to other galaxies and points in the universe. The amazing thing we found is that the jumps take no time. During the jump, no time passes, and we have no idea how this is possible. That's one of the things that convinced us that no matter how much knowledge you have, there is always room for more, like they say about Jell-O. Does any of this make sense?"

"I'm still trying to figure out the holographic televisions," I said.

They all laughed and said they were confused by many of the things that humans did, like watching professional wrestling and keeping pet rocks, and I told them I agreed with them.

Chapter Fifteen: Intergalactic

"We are near jump point," Fran said. "You don't need to do anything except be prepared because this jump is a little different than the last one."

Not knowing what being prepared was, I just sat still, and in a few minutes, the universe disappeared and reappeared several times, and the intervals were longer. In all, it was probably fewer than a couple of minutes. Then we were in a star system, but I noticed that the stars were a lot more scattered, and there seemed to be a lot less of them.

"Where are we?" I asked.

"We are in a small galaxy that is a companion to the Milky Way," Fran said. "It is called Carina by humans, and it's about two hundred eighty thousand light years as you measure. We are making a stop at a couple of planets just for show-and-tell. One is Earth-like, as it was a few billion years ago, and the other is more like Mars. We will need suits on both of them due to the oxygen levels. We will be at the first one in a few minutes, so everyone going landside needs to be getting suited."

Everyone but Fran got into suits, and we went through sterilization while waiting for the ship to land. We got out, and it looked a lot like Earth, except there wasn't much growing on the land but some mossy-looking stuff. There were a few tree stump–like things around the edge of the ocean, and I recognized them as stromatolites, the same type of things we have on Earth. They are like corals and are made from single-celled organisms. These are made in conjunction with the tides, so this planet must have a moon. Actually, it had four smaller moons that orbited in pairs. I had never seen anything like that before. We walked around and checked out the mossy stuff. Because it was green, I assumed it was photosynthetic and was told that I was right, but the O_2 level was about .005 percent at the current time. It would be a long time before aerobic creatures were here. We walked around, picked up a few things, looked at them, and put them back down. Every time we landed somewhere, I got such an urge to get samples and souvenirs, but I knew I would be taking a chance on contaminating Earth, so I abstained. Overall, there wasn't much excitement in comparison to what I had seen previously.

We got back on board and went through sterilizations as usual, and I was glad we didn't have to go through TSA every time we boarded.

The next planet was Mars-like, I was told, but it was in another star system in the galaxy. We made a small jump and were there. We got back into the suits and went through the procedures. When we got out this time, I saw small plants and even some type of insect-looking creatures. The planet didn't look red. It was desertlike, but there was quite a bit of water around. The O$_2$ levels were about 1 percent, so this was an improvement, but that wasn't capable of supporting people. There were weather systems, and we could see rain in the distance. It was also quite windy. This planet was much warmer and wetter than Mars is today. It looked like this Mars had a good chance of developing more life. I noticed some canyons and smoke in the distance from a volcano.

The little insect creatures didn't appear to have wings, but they had several pairs of legs and several types of greenery to live on. We watched them for a while, and I let one crawl over my glove. It looked soft-bodied, but it was hard to tell with the suit and gloves on.

After spending a few hours on this planet, we left. We were cruising when Milo asked, "Do you want to see another Earth-like planet that is more like Earth than any you have seen so far?"

"Of course," I said.

"It might be disturbing to you, so I want you to be prepared," said Milo.

"I don't think I can be surprised anymore than I have been already."

"We'll see," he responded.

The ship sped up, and we went through a long jump. I was told that we were in another small companion galaxy called the Small Magellanic Cloud, or SMC. It is in our local group but an irregular galaxy, and the planet we were starting to orbit looked an awful lot like Earth. There were satellites orbiting the planet, but they looked rather small and not very sophisticated. There were several continents, but they were not very connected.

Milo said, "We are going to have to wear suits here, but they are not for the atmosphere—they're for radiation. The inhabitants of this planet are very humanlike, and they developed nuclear power and then nuclear weapons, and then got into wars and used them. Each continent had its own religion and type of government, and of course, they were convinced they were the only one, and soon they started throwing nukes at each other, and now they are trying to hang on because the radiation is killing everything, including their food. They will be lucky to have enough beings to survive to keep the planet going. Right now, they are pretty much out of resources, so the war has ended because they are trying to survive. Most of the larger cities are gone, so they've regressed to a more agricultural lifestyle, except the radiation has harmed most everything, so the few isolated places not poisoned by radiation are making a living."

We started suiting up and went through sterilization. After we dressed, I asked why these suits were different.

"These aren't for O_2 levels but for radiation protection. The radiation level in most places is close to lethal. We will observe creatures in several different places," Milo said.

We got out and walked up a slight rise looking out over a fairly large city. The vegetation was sparse because either it was a nongrowing season or it had been killed by the radiation. It was nearly in total ruin. There was one bridge and a few partial buildings left, but there were creatures walking around. These creatures looked mostly like humans. However, they had compound eyes like insects instead of simple ones like we have. They didn't have hair on their heads, just a type of scales. You could see open sores on their arms and faces, probably from the radiation. They were rummaging through the ruins looking for things, but I don't know what. We watched them for a while and then returned to the ship.

We kept our suits on and took a short trip to a small village in a valley that was not destroyed. We got out, and Milo said we could take our helmets off. We again walked over to an observation point and watched the creatures. They seemed to be going through normal daily work. On the outskirts of town, there were blockades to stop them from leaving the valley. There appeared to be solar power and wind power on each building. There were large fields of crops of some kind, and there were smaller four-legged creatures, probably food animals, in pens. They looked mostly like goats but also had the compound eyes.

"Have the Vesi had contact with these creatures?" I asked.

Milo answered, "Yes, we did, but we abandoned the planet when the war started. As usual, the intelligent creatures we had contact with had no say in the way the planet was controlled. We thought the same thing was going to happen on Earth several decades ago, but it didn't, and we now think there is a chance for humans."

"Are there other planets like this?" I asked.

"Several that look almost the same," Milo said.

"One of the reasons we wanted to show you," he added.

"But I have no control over anything like this on Earth," I said.

"No, but maybe perhaps someone who does may read your book," he said.

"Couldn't you just bring one of them here and show him, and then maybe he could help them avoid it happening?" I asked.

"No. That would be a direct violation of our policy of influencing the humans."

"I suppose you're right, but it is a shame that we could advance so much if you all would help," I said.

Milo said, "As I said earlier, humans could do it themselves if they tried and didn't waste so much of their resources on war and other selfish endeavors."

It was time to go, and I would have loved to have some photos to show people, but I was sure that without the Vesi coming forth, nobody would believe any of it. For a few minutes, I wanted to slap all humans, and then I remembered that there were a heck of a lot of good ones in the bunch.

We got back in the ship and eased out of the atmosphere. We all sat back and relaxed after sterilization, just looking at stars for a few minutes. Then it was time for a snack. Packages were given out and opened, and they actually weren't bad. They were a lot like MREs the soldiers use, but probably more tasty. We finished them, and Milo said these planets were examples of the millions of ones that were inhabited.

"Are there other planets with technology like the Vesi have?" I asked.

"Thousands that we know of … and probably millions," Milo said.

"Will we be visiting any of them?" I asked.

"If you would like, but we are getting short on time for this trip, so we may have to make it later. There is also something we want you to see closer, but we'll have to wait for summer break for that. That is a closer view of a black hole. There is nothing more impressive in the universe than the event horizon," he continued.

"Also some closer looks at pulsars, quasars, supernova, and a few other things even we do not understand," added Fran.

"Why are you doing this, and why was I selected?" I asked.

"The short answer is that it's for your book mission," Milo said. "Another answer is that we actually like you, and we think that you are interested and capable of believing that this is real. Don't think that you are the only human that has viewed these things. You are just the first one who has been asked to say anything about it. Remember that it has almost zero chance of going any further. We have decided to take a chance of policy violation by doing this. The chances of success are so statically small that we are willing to risk this violation. We questioned whether we were in danger of taking on a human characteristic."

"What if I surprise you and become an enormous best seller and win awards, make millions, and have all humans looking for you?" I asked.

A collective laugh with looks of skepticism did not make me feel any better.

Milo asked, "Do you seriously think that a book without violence or sex will sell very well to humans? If we had figured that could possibly happen, we couldn't have proceeded with it. We have been surprised a couple of times by humans, but we are going with logic and past reactions to make our decisions.

"Some of the other human guests we have had were not able to change human life by large margins, but a few of Earth's great discoveries may have been made by some people who did see the technology," he said. "Even though you have seen our antigravity ships, how far could you get in trying to invent one or get someone to believe?"

"I see your point," I said. "I'll just write my book and have at least one copy for myself, which may be discovered centuries later, and somebody will say, 'Well, I'll be damned!'"

"Pretty much sums it up. As I've said, we're in no hurry at all," Milo said with a smile.

Chapter Sixteen: Milky Way Return

We started speeding up. Before long, we made a jump ... and another one a short time later. I assumed we were back into the Milky Way, and I was informed that I was right.

"We are returning to the earth's solar system from the other side that we left from," said Arrow. "We will see a few things we missed going the other way," he added. "We're going to pass a few of the TNOs, or trans-Neptunian objects, like Pluto and Sedna. There are lots of smaller ones that haven't been discovered yet by humans, but they will someday."

I could not pick out the sun from that distance, and as we approached the first one, I could see that it looked like a dirty snowball but was quite large. I was told that it hadn't been discovered yet, but it was numbered Sun-23, as the twenty-third planet, or planetoid, orbiting the sun. The earth was Sun-3. The moon was designated Sun-3.1. We then went on to Sedna. Sedna was reddish compared to the other TNOs. Of course, the one I wanted to see was Pluto. Not too much later, we arrived at Pluto and slowed to get a good look at it and its moon, Charon.

I felt somewhat sorry for Pluto, realizing that in the universe, it was rather insignificant. Then I realized how insignificant the earth was and felt somewhat scared and then disappointed. Then I realized how happy I was just knowing these things.

"Just to make it easier," Fran said, "we are going to cruise back so that we arrive in the middle of the night on the North American East Coast. This would be a good time to look at those history cubes you brought—unless you'd rather nap."

"I'd forgotten I brought them," I said. "I'd love to look at each of them for a few minutes, just to get acquainted with the times, but I can't hold much more knowledge because I am totally on overload."

"I understand," she said. "Crash, would you take Mac to the viewing room and show him how to operate the viewer?"

"*Jawohl* … I mean, sure, I would be glad to," said Craig.

He motioned for me to follow, and we went to a viewing room about the size of a small personal theater. There was a console in the middle of the room, and my two cubes were there. Crash showed me how to install them. It just involved setting them in and closing the top. He showed me how to use the joystick to advance or rewind the scene. I selected the date and time. The picture on the screen was a lot like the view of Earth on Google Earth. I could zoom in to where I wanted to go and then keep zooming in on cities, buildings, and even see inside the buildings and rooms. I could not believe how much information was recorded on one little cube.

I zoomed in on Philadelphia and zeroed in on September 5, 1774, finding Carpenters' Hall. It was easy to find since Philly was small in comparison to today. I zoomed inside and pressed the button on the joystick. The room opened all around me, and it looked as if I were in the middle of it. The first thing I noticed was the smell. I asked Crash what the smoky body odor smell was.

"That's humanity when baths were a weekly affair at best. Those clothes were aired out, but they were mostly wool, and wool wasn't washed much, if at all. The smoky smell was, of course, the wood and coal-fired heat and cooking sources. Right Guard was not even a football lineman at that time." He laughed.

"Sometimes I don't know if I'm so happy that you could record smells also," I said.

Crash said, "I know what you mean. Wait until you go back to the Middle Ages. You'll find out why they started burying flowers with their loved ones. The main reason wasn't for love. It was the same thing for weddings. The reason the bride carried flowers will become obvious, along with the reason that weddings were held in the spring. That was when most people got their baths. With the flowers and a bath, June became a big wedding month. The Neanderthals started burying their dead with flowers before the Cro-Magnons even started. The latter probably adopted the custom from them.

"I'm going to leave and let you explore your cube," Crash said. "If you need any assistance, just say the word and someone will come help you."

Crash left, and I went back to looking around the room, seeing if there was somebody I might recognize. I did recognize, from paintings of them, of course, Thomas Jefferson, George Washington, John Adams, Ben Franklin, and Patrick Henry. The others I could only guess at. Washington was tall for the group—most of the others seemed to be slightly less than six feet tall—but he didn't look too healthy to me. He appeared to have teeth problems, but as best I could tell, they were not wooden. Moreover, he wasn't wearing a wig, but he'd had something done to his hair. As I was listening to them all complain about the taxes and rules the king had put forth, I noticed that they were talking like modern people do.

Immediately I said, "Assistance, please."

In a minute, Milo came in, and I asked him why they sounded like modern Americans rather than using older English.

Milo said with a chuckle, "We should have mentioned that. Since there is quite a bit of difference between the dialects, your translators treat the old English as they would any foreign language. That's why you should remember to turn them off back on Earth unless you need them. If you turn them off now, you'll hear the old English. It'll get on your nerves after a few minutes, but it is entertaining."

"Thanks," I said. "I should have thought of that myself."

Still chuckling, Milo left, and when I thought about it, it was rather funny. I was too tired to get into a lengthy viewing of the proceedings. I wanted to have ample time to listen to arguments about guns, taxes, and all that stuff. People and the Supreme Court are always saying they know what our forefathers meant. I had a strong feeling that we had no idea what they discussed, much less meant. I thought I would change cubes and go to the time around the birth of Jesus to see if anything was as we say it was.

I switched cubes and zoomed in to the Middle East. I had no idea where I might find Jesus.

"Assistance, please," I said. Within a minute, Milo was back and, I explained my dilemma.

Milo said, "Yes, we have had to help humans do this before. Anything in particular?"

"I just wanted to see what Jesus and the area looked like in those days."

Milo started adjusting the viewer. "Okay, I'm going to take you to a time when he was just starting to go around with his disciples. That way you can see some of them also. How's that?"

"Perfect," I said.

Milo zoomed into the place and time and pressed the button. "You have to realize that we are limited in how much we have recorded there. We weren't doing much recording in that part of the world until everything started happening," Milo said. "If you want to know about virgin birth, we don't know. Scientifically, we would doubt it, but stranger things have happened."

Suddenly we were in a group of people listening to a man speaking. This time, I didn't need to ask why there were speaking modern English instead of Aramaic. The man speaking was definitely not a blue-eyed blond. He was slender and looked quite strong. He looked very Jewish with an olive complexion and dark eyes. I knew that he was Jesus, and wondered if modern Christians would accept him. He talked about how right it is to help other people, even your enemies. I knew that this wouldn't go over too well with a lot of people now. I noticed that people carried very few possessions. This was more or less how I had pictured Jesus in my mind. I decided that I would have to come back for a longer viewing of that particular time. I was too tired to pay much attention to what was going on.

I noted the times and latitude and longitude coordinates, took out the cube, and left the theater. Going to one of the cots, I lay down and immediately dropped off to sleep. I must have slept hard because after a couple of hours, I was awake and refreshed and went back into the control room. In the viewer, I could see the earth getting larger, and the sun was quite large as compared to before.

"We're going to do a slow sterilization, so you may occasionally feel a little tingle, but it is a more thorough procedure," Fran said. "We do these when we've been on multiple planets, just in case there's some new life form we might have overlooked. If it gets through the sterilization process, then we probably couldn't stop it anyway. We did once pick one up on an obscure planet, and it actually thrived on the sterilization energy. We ended up having to have another ship come rescue us. When I say us, I mean the other Vesi. I was not on board for that one. We sent our ship into the sun for destruction after we were sure the Vesi were cleared and on board the rescue ship. And we hate to lose an intergalactic ship."

We were into an orbit now and just waiting for the right time of night to reenter. It was fantastic watching the darkness progress across the globe. The edge of darkness was now in the middle of the Atlantic and slowly going toward the East Coast of North America. The lights in Europe were interesting, as was the absence of them in some other parts of the world.

Actually, I was getting anxious to get back to reality as most of us know it, and I didn't know how I could ever watch a UFO program or a science fiction program without thinking, *If you only knew.*

Before long, it was dark where we needed it to be, and we reentered, going into the Caribbean and back to the home base. Milo asked if I could spend the night, as they would like to talk to me later about the mission, kind of like a debriefing. I agreed, and we went for a snack and then to get some sleep. I didn't know what time or day it was, so I checked and found that I only had two days of Christmas—excuse me, winter—break left. Time was different when you were having fun and traveling around at light speed. Time actually went slower for us than it did on Earth.

I showered—why, I didn't know—and went to bed. I woke after about four hours. I realized that I'd had only had about six or eight hours of sleep over the entire two weeks of break, but it was only a few days in space. I would have to get used to this space/speed/time thing.

If anyone asked me if I went anywhere over break, I didn't know what I would say. I thought I might tell some of the other teachers just to see their reactions.

Chapter Seventeen: Debriefing

I dressed, went to the closest cafeteria, and got some coffee and a small breakfast sandwich. I was just thinking about what we had done and seen on this trip when *all* the crews came in and joined me. There was also an elderly gentleman with them. When I say elderly, I mean that he looked elderly by Earth standards. Milo introduced him as Julius. We all moved to a larger table that had been set up for us. Everyone ordered something light, and we started chatting about the trip.

"This is like a debriefing, and we want to make sure that there aren't any lingering questions," Milo said. "We also want to see how you feel about things up to this point."

"Was this like a standard trip or was it custom made?" I asked.

Fran replied, "It was custom made to fit into the time frame here on Earth—and to include a small sample of the things to expect. There are millions of inhabited planets in the Milky Way alone. Thousands have intelligent life on them, and hundreds have space travel. Several have intergalactic travel and so forth. Once you get out of the Milky Way, the numbers are astronomical. Very few intelligent species are dangerous. Most intelligent species we have encountered are like us, in search of knowledge and interested in how other creatures develop."

I asked, "Have other species like the Vesi been on Earth before?"

"Yes," said Milo. "About sixty thousand years ago, Earth time, another group much like us landed here and put up a colony. We met them, and after discussing things, they decided to leave and let us continue. They had left from a nova star, just as we had. It is amazing how similar things happen, and how groups evolve alike—parallel evolution gone wild."

"I'm still amazed at how hominoid the intelligent species seem to be," I said. "Even the Insecteriams had the same basic design."

117

"Of course, most of the ones that come here are looking for this type of planet, so it's only natural that many of the same characteristics develop. Once in a great while, a scout ship will come here and do environmental tests, going back to report or take samples. There's only one time we can remember that a ship landed in Central America and ended up capturing the entire population and leaving with them."

"That might explain some things, like the disappearance of some cultures from Central and South America," I said.

"They lived with the group for several years and then left with them," said Milo. "We don't know where they were from because we decided not to contact them since they had direct contact and influence with the group. It might have violated our policy, but we wished it had never happened. I guess they didn't think the natives were intelligent since they didn't have electricity or outside communications. They just disappeared."

"You realize that it is hard to believe that humans could turn out like the Vesi," I said.

"Actually, there are lots of people on Earth that have the same sort of attitudes, but they never end up in positions of power because it isn't compatible with your systems of governments," Fran said. "But there is hope that attitudes may change. Anything on these trips that made you feel uneasy or troubled?"

"I was a little bothered at first with the abduction. All things considered, it wasn't that bad. Actually, I had fun, but probably would not have if I'd been one of the abductees."

"How do you feel about humans planning to return to the moon?" Stretch asked.

"Personally, I think it's a total waste of money, except for maybe the development of new hardware in the area of rockets and computers and so on," I replied. "At such a prohibitive cost, there isn't anything special enough to go there for."

"What about Mars?" she asked.

"The main reason humans want to go to Mars is to see if there is any kind of life there," I said. "This can be done with robots, making it safer, quicker, easier, and less expensive. Of course, humans want to go for the adventure, but I now have a different view of it. The trip out of the solar system was tremendous, but I still have a hard time getting it all to fit into my little brain."

Crash said, "You realize we could have faked the whole thing, like the moon landing, don't you?"

"The moon landing was faked?" I asked.

They all just laughed.

"No," Arrow said. "That was just a joke. In fact, we actually were along with your craft from a distance, but we didn't assist in any way. The last thing we tampered with was the 2004 Florida presidential election, and after that, we learned to stay out of the way." Arrow laughed. I knew he was just kidding, or was he?

Julius, who had just been observing, finally spoke. "What do you think of the Vesi as a group?"

"I am extremely impressed with the technology and most of the philosophy," I answered. "I just wish I could share it with the rest of the humans. Which brings up another question: Have any humans tried to use anything they saw here topside?"

Julius replied, "There have been very few humans down here. It is rare when someone is invited, so you should feel good about that. I've been happy with our choice so far. It was a hard decision, and that is why I wanted to get involved. As you can tell, I am a little longer in the tooth, as humans say. I've been here since your Middle Ages, so I've seen many changes for humans, including the discovery of electricity, which was your biggest change. It was around a long time before Ben Franklin was even born, but there wasn't a single moment when it popped up. It was a slow discovery. Also, I won't say for sure, but if you look at the helicopter Leonardo da Vinci drew, it sure looks like the flying insects from the Triad planet." Then he gave me a smile that I swear looked like the one on the *Mona Lisa*. I really needed a rest.

"Do you have any problems with your mission—anything you think will be too hard or unethical?" Julius asked.

"I don't think it will be too hard or unethical, but I don't see a lot of people buying the book," I answered.

"We don't expect many people to either. We're just interested in the correct one or two persons getting some ideas and maybe starting some work on things. We are in no hurry, as you can tell."

"As we say, I'll give it the old college try," I said.

"That's all we ask. Feel free to visit anytime—and for as long as you wish. Who knows? Maybe someday you may decide to correct some misrepresentations of history by using the cubes. Stranger things have happened."

Then Julius took a deep breath and said, "You know, humans have advanced at a great pace in the last two to three thousand years. Especially the last hundred years or so. But you don't realize that you are subject to elimination from several possible sources other than yourselves: one meteorite of the correct size, one virus of the wrong type, one solar flare of the wrong type, loss of your ozone layer, and so forth. And that's not to mention what you are doing to your environment. We really have hope for you all and look forward to seeing some positive progress as a species. I would bet, if we did bet, you will succeed. I probably won't be around to see it, but most of these other Vesi will. There isn't that much time to either get started in the right direction or humans may fail as a species. I wish you and your fellow Earthlings well in your future endeavors, and who knows, you could remotely be responsible for a little bit of it."

He reached out and shook my hand, and the strangest feeling came over me. I was proud of humans and myself—and at the same time scared to death for the human race and myself.

"Thank you very much, I think," I said. Julius just gave me a nice smile.

"Well, it's time to get you back before it gets too light, and so you can get some rest before you have to go back to work," Fran said. "Are there any final requests before we say good-bye until the next time?"

"Just one thing," I said with a laugh. "Since I like to fish, may I borrow your translator so I can get hold of Sam when I go out fishing? It would save me a lot of work."

Everyone laughed, and we all walked back to the small hangar to say our good-byes. Within an hour, I was back, walking into my house, where Ralph and Hide and Seek came to meet me. Ralph acted as if it was the happiest day of his life. Hide and Seek acted as if they couldn't care less, looking at me as if trying to determine whether I'd brought any special treats that they might possibly eat if they smelled just right. However, they did come to bed, honoring me with their presence. They let me know in the morning that they were available for petting if I had missed that while I was away.

I spent the weekend getting ready to go back to work. I had next semester to get started on, but every time I started doing something, my mind drifted off to the things that I had seen. It was just terrible not being able to tell anyone. Then I realized that I actually would get to tell everyone in the world. It was just unlikely that folks would read about it, and then I wondered if those who did would care.

Monday came, and it was the usual zoo at school. Most of the classes were disorganized because the students had been out for a couple of weeks. They all had to catch up on their social lives. My first astronomy class was just starting when one of the students raised his hand and voice and started yelling, "Mr. Mac, Mr. Mac, did you see the thing on CNN about the UFO over Bethlehem during Christmas break? Do you think it was real? Do you think they were there because of Christmas?"

The entire class laughed aloud and started talking, of course.

I just smiled and said to myself, *If they only knew …*

About the Author

Harry Truman Flynn was born and raised in the small town of Science Hill, Kentucky. As a child, he was always interested in science. He attended Eastern Kentucky University for a brief time before joining the U.S. Air Force. While in the military, he worked on air-to-air missiles and was stationed in Denver, Colorado, and Aviano, Italy. Upon his discharge, he became a hardware support specialist on large mainframe computers and lived in Lexington, Kentucky; Frankfurt, Germany; and Tampa, Florida. After twenty years, he tired of the travel and returned to college. He graduated from the University of South Florida with teacher certifications in biology and chemistry. He taught high school biology and chemistry in Tampa.

He and his wife, Irene, have two children, Michael and Erin. They also have three cats and a dog. They enjoy their butterfly garden and attracting birds to their yard in Tampa.

Interested in science throughout his life, Harry decided to write about some of the ideas he's had over the years ... and some of the things he envisions for the future.